·ROMA NOVA·
EXTRA

ALISON MORTON

Pulcheria
Press

Published in 2018 by Pulcheria Press
Copyright © 2018 by Alison Morton
All rights reserved Tous droits réservés

The right of Alison Morton to be identified as the author of this work has been asserted in accordance with the Copyright, Designs and Patents Acts 1988 Sections 77 and 78.

No part of this book may be reproduced, stored in a retrieval system or transmitted in any form or by any means, electronic, mechanical, photocopying, recording or otherwise, without prior written permission of the copyright holder, except for the use of brief quotations in a book review.

Propriété littéraire d'Alison Morton
Tous droits de reproduction, d'adaptation et de traduction, intégrale ou partielle réservés pour tous pays. L'auteur ou l'éditeur est seul propriétaire des droits et responsable du contenu de ce livre.

Le Code de la propriété intellectuelle interdit les copies ou reproductions destinées à une utilisation collective. Toute représentation ou reproduction intégrale ou partielle faite par quelque procédé que ce soit, sans le consentement de l'auteur ou de ses ayant droit ou ayant cause, est illicite et constitue une contrefaçon, aux termes des articles L.335-2 et suivants du Code de la propriété intellectuelle

This is a work of fiction. Names, characters, places, incidents are either products of the author's imagination or used fictitiously. Any resemblance to actual events, locales or persons living or dead is entirely coincidental.

ISBN 9791097310103

DRAMATIS PERSONAE

Mitela family
Gaius Mitelus – Fourth century Roman senator
Galla Mitela – Eleventh century councillor and envoy
Carina Mitela – Junior head/head of Mitela clan, ex-Praetorian Guard Special Forces (PGSF) officer
Conradus Mitelus – 'Conrad', Carina's husband, ex-PGSF officer
Aurelia Mitela – Carina's grandmother
Allegra Mitela – Carina's and Conrad's eldest daughter
Antonia and Gillius – 'Tonia' and 'Gil', twins, Carina and Conrad's younger children
Helena Mitela – Carina's cousin

Household
Junia Sestina – Steward of Domus Mitelarum
Galienus – Under-steward/housekeeper
Macrinus – Junia's son, and later under-steward

Military
Daniel Stern – PGSF officer
Flavius – Optio, later centurion, PGSF
Sergilia – Centurion, PGSF detail in Rome
Diana Sergilia – Sergilia's daughter, Lieutenant, PGSF

Apulius family
Lucius Apulius – Roman tribune, later senator
Julia Bacausa – Daughter of Celtic prince Bacausus in Roman Noricum
Julia Apulia – Lucius and Julia's (wayward) daughter
Claudia Apulia – Eleventh century descendant
Silvia Apulia – Lucius's sixty-fifth-generation descendant

Tellus family
Caius Tellus (deceased) – Unsavoury rebel

Other
Bacausus – Celtic prince, Roman Noricum
Titus Calavius – Tribune, Danube frontier, later veteran in Rome
Gilbert de Boscville – Annoying Norman at Duke William's court
Eadmær – Saxon, attached to King Harold's court
Andrea Luca – Italian architect
Sextilius Gavro – 'Mad inventor' cousin of Conrad
Dolcia Plicata – Tax inspector from the Censor's office

Historically recorded people
Count Theodosius – Fourth century 'fixer' for Emperor Valentinian
Emperor Theodosius – Count Theodosius's son
Matilda and William of Normandy

PART I
GLIMPSES FROM HISTORY

AD 370

Lucius Apulius, a young military tribune, is posted to the back end of the empire as Rome struggles to keep the barbarians behind the Danube. There Apulius meets the fiery Julia Bacausa under most unusual circumstances.

THE GIRL FROM THE MARKET

Virunum, Roman Noricum AD 370

Her eyes. That's what drew me. Almond shaped, yet full at their widest, and blue like the Mare Nostrum lapping at the shore by my grandmother's villa at Baiae. The red hair piled up on her head, gold laced artfully between the strands. Amber drops fell from her ears and nearly met the white curved flesh of her shoulders and touched the heavy rope of amber and gold circling her neck.

Gods.

The Celtic princeling we were visiting coughed. 'May I present my daughter, Julia Bacausa?'

I was no fresh-minted tribune but a company commander, heading my own troops for a full season, but I was staring at her as if I was an unemancipated adolescent. The civil governor and the Celt talked about local affairs as they led the way to the dining room. The girl walking silently by her father. Fingers grasping my arm pulled me back into the real world.

'Don't even think about it, young Apulius,' Opsius, the local military commander, hissed as we left the atrium. 'Not unless you want to be impaled through your arse, praying for death out on a freezing mountain. Come on, let's get our dinner. I'm starving.'

But it was already too late. She was the girl from the market.

Britannia, a year earlier

I was serving on Count Theodosius's staff, eager as any young officer to reimpose Roman rule after the barbarian conspiracy. We'd smashed the predatory bands who'd looted their way across the colony and restored property to the traumatised inhabitants, less our cut. Gods, their pale faces and pathetic thanks, their hands touching us and words praising us made us feel like noble heroes of old.

Then that damned Pannonian exile Valentinus got up to his old tricks again, rising against Theodosius when he landed in Britannia by organising fellow exiles and attempting to bribe local troops to his cause. Well, we had him now. Theodosius handed him over to Dulcitius, the new *dux Britanniarum* who carried out a cursory investigation into Valentinus's rebellion and shortly after that executed him.

My promotion came quickly after the end of that campaign; the count promised me my own new independent command in the West and I couldn't wait to set off. But the clerks insisted they had to process their paperwork. To say I was impatient was an understatement, but in the interim I was attached to Count Theodosius's headquarters staff where I could observe how the great man developed and organised his strategy. Then that bastard Dulcitius spotted me.

Tall, sturdy and imposing in his full uniform, and helmet clasped under his left arm, he'd walked into Theodosius's tent as if it were his. But he saluted the count respectfully enough. He'd come to bid a formal farewell to Theodosius before travelling to take up his post in the north.

I'd been curious to see Dulcitius in person. Said to be an excellent soldier and a commander with a hard reputation, he'd been thrown out of the army by the late Emperor Julian. Why had Count Theodosius summoned him back? Dulcitius scanned the tent with his dark flashing eyes, nodding at two of the other officers. Then he stopped at me.

'Aren't you General Apulius's son?' Dulcitius growled and jabbed his finger at me. 'That pagan who crawled away from Samarra after Julian the Apostate's death?'

The whole tent fell silent. Count Theodosius looked up from his dispatch. A secretary shuffled scrolls in the background. And all eyes focused on me. Christian eyes.

'What exactly are you saying, Dulcitius?' The count leaned back in his chair.

'He's from one of those useless aristo families that Diocletian chucked out.'

'Maybe so, but he's one of my most promising juniors who's led several very successful sorties.' The count turned to me. 'Lucius?'

'Sir, I've served the emperor for six years to the utmost of my ability, and completely loyally.' I burned inside with fury at the new *dux*, but kept my eyes on Theodosius.

'Ask him who he worships.' Dulcitius looked at me malevolently.

In the week it took to arrange my posting to a low-level auxiliary troop in the middle of nowhere, my colleagues drifted away, little by little. Conversations about the campaign – the thing that bound us together – stopped when I was near. Pity, embarrassment, even fear of contamination. Count Theodosius called me into the staff tent the morning I left.

'Sure you won't think again? It's a small thing you have to do – half an hour a week chanting a few prayers. Nobody's going to ask what you're really thinking.'

I'd glimpsed the count at his prayers, but always in the company of others. Perhaps he was a less enthusiastic Christian than he appeared in public.

'You're a good soldier, Apulius,' he continued, 'with potential to become a great one and a leader of men. Who knows, these days you may even attain the purple as emperor. Don't let pig-headedness ruin your career.' He slammed his palm down on the table. 'Even the damned Goths have converted.' He glared at me and snorted.

'Sir, it's still legal to practise one's religion privately. I don't seek to make anybody give up their sincere beliefs, whatever I may think of them.'

'Perhaps so, but if that boy prig Gratian takes over after Valentinian, you'll be lucky to escape alive.' He shrugged. 'You're a fool not to see what's coming.'

I said nothing, but stood to attention waiting to be dismissed.

'Get on your way then. And good luck. I doubt we'll meet again.'

Typical of autumn in Britannia, it rained all the way to Dubris, then during the crossing to Bononia and through the northern part of Gaul. I slumped on my horse, my leather poncho keeping most of the water off. But it was heavy, and clammy inside. At least the wagon with its leather covering was keeping most of my possessions dry. I only hoped my books in my locked chest survived the humidity. The driver and relief driver sitting behind him on the box stared ahead and flicked the reins from time to time with no expression on their faces.

Ascus, my servant, never the most cheerful soul, slouched on his mule and grumbled all the way. He had a unique talent for finding the worst repaired roads and the muddiest courtyards at wayside inns. Luckily, the drivers always overruled him with their local knowledge and we mostly stayed at official *mansiones* – bare, but adequate for a military officer on his way to a new posting. Most of the time. But at Vesantio, once we'd driven down the interminable slope towards the town, the drivers refused to risk their wagon further east despite the regular military patrols.

'Augusta Raurica? No chance. Too near the frontier, legate,' the older one said with a smirk. 'Good luck with that,' he said as he and his mate dumped my belongings in the courtyard of the *mansio* by the city walls. I was forced to fork out for mules. Ascus surprised me for once and returned with four healthy specimens, complete with pack saddles.

'Nobody would hire them. I had to buy them, and the leather panniers on the wood frames, so there's no change.' He looked down.

I held out my hand and waited. He slowly dug his fingers into his waist pouch and brought out a gold *solidus*, one *miliarense* and some *folles*. If he'd been honest, I would have given him them as a reward. I made up my mind there and then I was fed up with his tricks. I would sell him when I reached Virunum.

Crisp mornings with a slow sun replaced the rain, thank Mars, and we passed an agreeable three days at the fort at Augusta Raurica. I volunteered as duty officer on Sunday to escape the Galilean service. I was surprised to be accompanied on my rounds by one of the other tribunes, a newly minted thin-striper called Titus Calavius.

'Looks quiet, doesn't it, sir?' He pointed to the River Rhenus that wound like a grey-brown snake below us and then to the wooded hills opposite. 'But those Alemanni bastards are just waiting. One day they'll pour out of the woods screaming, and tear across the river.' He shivered. 'But we'll be ready. Then we'll push them back and recover Germania Superior!'

I laid my hand on his shoulder. He couldn't have been more than seventeen. I felt old at twenty-five beside him. I didn't have the heart to tell him that despite his passion and courage, he'd probably be running the other way on that day.

His exaggerated optimism must have grated on the more seasoned officers and soldiers, hardened in fighting and able to see that Rome wasn't the force it had been. Perhaps getting him out of their hair for a few days was the reason he was given command of my escort along the *limes* to Brigantium then Cambodunum.

Titus Calavius was a good-hearted lad from a traditional senatorial family in Rome. With his fire and patriotism, he would have thrived two centuries ago. Now he was at the dead end of the Roman world. He chatted enthusiastically as we rode towards Brigantium, asking me about my time in Britannia. I tried to keep the sour note out of my words. I waved yet another customs agent with a greedy gleam in his eye away from my possessions as I crossed my fifth provincial border, this time into Raetia, and Titus glowered with a good Roman soldier's scorn at the agent.

In Brigantium we were billeted in Valentinian's new harbour fortress; it was rough and ready, a proper frontier post, but Ascus laid out bedrolls then made an effort to find where the baths were located. Perhaps I wouldn't sell him after all. Looking out onto the still lake after supper with the naval commander, a cup of wine in my hand, it was hard to think that barbarians were in the low hills opposite, planning their strategy to destroy everything Roman. From what I'd seen, the frontier fort system, the *limes*, was impressive and the garrisons determined. Of course, as well as fighting for Rome, they were trying to keep their own skins attached to their bodies – a good motivator.

The next morning, we assembled an hour before dawn, reinforced by six local troops.

'Sorry I can't give you more cover, tribune,' the prefect said and extended his hand to me. His frown emphasised the harsh lines of his face, topped with one inch of greying hair. 'These raiding parties of barbarians between here and Cambodunum are a fucking nuisance.' He eyed up my little convoy. 'Keep close and don't let those bloody mules stop for anything. You have a hard day of riding. *Bona fortuna!*'

'Thank you, sir,' I said. Six months later I heard he'd been killed fending off one of those raiding parties.

Twelve hours later, we trudged up the hill to the defensive fort of Cambodunum, a pig of an ascent. Three sets of grumpy guards challenged us – a perfect end to a tense day. We'd been shadowed by barbarians, fought through an ambush and were sweating and filthy, desperate for the baths.

'Just direct me to the *praetorium* and get out of my bloody way,' I snapped at the last pair.

Clean, fed and rested, I nodded when the prefect, a studious, boring man, recounted that the old town had been sacked by the Alemanni two centuries ago and the fort had been rebuilt on the highest point around. He would have talked all night. Titus and I made a change from the monotonous conversation of the local town councillors, he said. I was stifling yawns by then, but agreed they had a job I wouldn't wish on the devils in Tartarus. I stayed another two nights there to recuperate our spirits and more importantly let my animals recover their strength.

But Titus Calavius left the next morning with his escort to return to Augusta Raurica.

'I've enjoyed your company, Titus, as well as your troop's protection,' I said. 'Convey my thanks to the prefect. If you're ever in Virunum, or even Rome, look me up. You'll always be welcome in the house of Apulius.'

'Thank you, sir. The pleasure and the duty were mine.' I looked at his young face, now solemn. His helmet looked too large for him, but his spine was straight as he sat on the fidgeting horse. He wheeled round and they trotted off out of the fort gate. I wondered if he would make it back to Augusta.

Ascus and I wound our way along the Via Julia, the salt road to Iuvavum. Messengers from the *cursus publicus* thundered by on horseback now and again, which startled the Hades out of our mules. Carts and wagons, groups of civilians, occasional troops of hard-faced *limitanei* clattered along behind and in front of us. But something I was totally unprepared for was the magnificent scenery. Higher than the Apennines, and more dramatic than anything I'd seen in Britannia, their white peaks and green uplands under a clear azure sky mesmerised me. It was the type of place where you could be at peace, away from frontier struggles, religious hatred, politicking and endless self-seeking. I drew a long breath in. Maybe this posting wouldn't be as bad as I thought.

Iuvavum, surrounded by hills, looked idyllic but it was congested, noisy and stank. No regular military were based here to keep order, and it showed. People looked prosperous enough, but the constant jostling and shouting was annoying, not least from the shops and stalls. Quick darting children, almost feral, sly pickpockets, women with no soul left in their eyes touting their bodies mixed in with the more prosperous citizens. I could have been in the Subura in Rome.

After we fought our way through the crowds to cross the bridge, the air became clearer and more gracious buildings appeared on each side of the road. The gods help us if Virunum was like this.

Next morning, rain descended on the town. Lightning ran around the hills between the dark grey clouds. Ascus pulled my poncho out of one of the packs and handed it to me with a look of reproach. Mine was a *paenula scortea*, leather and waterproof; his was only wool, but it was thick and close woven. He'd survive.

We took a further week rambling through mountain valleys. The local guide I'd hired said there was a more direct route over the mountains, but only just passable with a train of pack animals like ours at this time of the year as the snow was still deep up there. And who knew what brigands were lying in wait for an isolated traveller, he said, glancing at me. So I opted to join the main route from Ovilava to Virunum which at least carried official traffic. But a week later, it was still raining; cold, dripping rain that soaked any part of your skin exposed. The *mansiones* provided some relief and at least our poor beasts were under shelter, but the rain and mountain mist became depressing. I thought when I left Britannia I'd also left perpetual dampness behind. To top it all, when I'd arrived in Virunum, it had been snowing. After reporting in to the military commander and given a billet in his house, I drank myself to sleep that night.

Virunum

Within a week, I was screaming with boredom. As the second in command, I was responsible for the men's fighting efficiency. I had the centurions drill them to exhaustion, we mounted simulated attacks, we practised covert recce drills. But nothing. The fifth large-scale sortie I'd led, this time down the road south to Aquileia which had to be kept open at all costs, and we hadn't found a single insurgent. Jupiter curse all barbarians to Hades.

Virunum and the whole province of Noricum Mediterraneum were critical for supplying the army with weapons of all kinds – a sword made from the famous Noricum steel wielded by one soldier would bring gleams of envy in the eyes of his tentmates. But my biggest battles were settling squabbles between merchants, especially between the local ones and those on the way to the Amber Road, and breaking up more serious fights between groups of drunken blacksmiths and their workers spending their money in the bars.

I threw the reins of my horse to the groom and strode off in the direction of the market, a known centre of shifty characters. Catching one of them would ease my temper as the exercise would ease my aching backside.

Then I saw the girl. She was pawing through bowls and plates on a stall manned by a Gaul with drooping red moustaches and a pained smile. Her hands waved to reinforce her argument, causing the sleeve of her dull brown robe to fall back and reveal slender, shapely arms sprinkled with freckles.

'Is this man cheating you?' I said to her.

'What business is it of yours?' She looked me up and down with a damned insolent air. Gods, she was another bloody provincial semi-barbarian with a plait of red hair. She wore no jewellery; her belt was plain leather without a waist pouch and her tunic didn't even cover her feet and ankles. A pert farm girl, or somebody's household slave who had the nerve to measure me up like an equal. But she was worth looking at, I had to admit.

'None,' I said and turned away.

'Wait, Roman.'

I was already moving and ignored her.

'I said wait!'

I walked on. I didn't take orders from peasants, especially impertinent ones. The next moment, strong fingers gripped my arm. I looked down at a clean, white hand with no ring. Indoor slave, then.

'Nobody turns his back and walks away from me.'

'How dare you touch me! Remove your hand or I'll have you whipped.'

'You can't.'

'We'll see about that.' I started to raise my hand to summon two of my detail, but her sparkling eyes made me catch my breath. Her face and neck were flushed and her face tipped up, defying me. Whether she was slave or free, her master was bloody lucky to have her on tap. But I bet she was the proverbial handful in bed.

Meanwhile I'd teach her a lesson to remember her place. I prised her fingers off, grabbed her wrist and pulled her to me.

'You have no right,' she snapped.

'You refuse me, a Roman officer?' I said and pulled her round the corner where I pushed her against the wall and hitched her tunic up, sliding my hand between her legs.

She gasped, and stared at me with those bright blue eyes. A flash of emotion ran through them. Anger? Surprise? Her shoulders slumped as she leant back against the rough stone of the wall, her back arched. She said nothing, I waited for her to pull against my grip, but she didn't make the least struggle. All she did was tilt her head up and look down her nose at me, searching my face. She didn't even blink. Was she simple-minded? Then she half closed her eyes and her lips parted as she took a breath.

'You have to pay,' she said. Her voice was low, harsh like granite.

A tart, then.

I left her upstairs in the *caupona* afterwards, three gold *solidi* on the stool beside the bed. I paid the bartender for the room and returned to my billet well satisfied; those legs and tits, and when we'd come I thought I'd flown to Elysium. But her eyes. You'd think she had a soul.

Now, only days later, I was reclining on a padded couch in her father's house with the governor and Opsius, the military commander, listening to lyre music and soft singing as if we were in a civilised city. Around us, servants flitted in and out as efficiently as the best in Rome. The walls were covered in superb frescoes, bordered by heavy crimson and gold edged curtains. Flames from sconces flickered with a strong yellow light and gave out a sweet almond scent.

But I was sweating, terrified and waiting for the girl to drop the few words that would precipitate my excruciatingly painful death. She made the occasional comment to the governor or her father, but none across the central table to either of us military men. I was mesmerised by a curl of red hair attempting to escape from the gold band just above her ear. I wanted to run my fingers into the hollows at the base of her neck and hear her sigh with pleasure. Again. And over her stomach and further…

'So have you settled into our town, tribune?' the Celt asked politely, a hint of a smile on his lips as if he knew exactly what was going through my mind.

I swallowed hard.

'I have my billet and my duties, sir,' I replied. 'I hope to see some action soon, though.'

'You young men always want to kill other young men.' The older man sighed. 'Argentoratum with Julian in '57 was enough for me.'

'You fought against Emperor Julian?'

He burst out laughing. 'You really *do* think we're barbarians!'

The girl glared at me, the military commander jerked upright and the governor frowned. Even the lyre player stopped. Only a muted spitting from the brazier broke the silence.

'Apologise this instant, Apulius,' Opsius growled at me after a few seconds. 'You're talking out of your arse.' He glanced at the girl. 'Begging your pardon, noble lady.'

She nodded graciously, then fixed her hard blue stare on me again.

'Prince Bacausus served in the emperor's *palatini*,' Opsius added.

Mars save me, the elite regiments in the army, with a fearsome combat reputation. Even if I managed to escape tonight with a whole skin, I'd sealed the end of my career. I stood, nodded to the two Romans and bowed to the Celt.

'Please forgive my error, prince. I was crass. I beg your leave to withdraw.'

'Well said, young man,' he replied, his eyes assessing me. 'At least you have the balls to apologise when you're wrong.' He flicked his fingers at me. 'Go and get some fresh air. Julia will show you the garden.'

She tightened her mouth and jaw, but her father waved her on. As we left the dining room, no back could have been stiffer. She looked straight ahead, chin in the air. A middle-aged woman, presumably her body slave, tagged along barely three feet behind us.

The girl led me through a paved area then on to a gravel path lined with torches and box hedges containing a surprising variety of colourful shrubs and trees. But flowers were the furthest thing from my terrified mind. As we strolled along, I could say nothing. Even a full apology, prostrated on the ground wouldn't be enough. I'd brought disgrace on my father and on Rome, but most of all, I'd dishonoured this vibrant creature and her father. I closed my eyes for a second. I would ride out tomorrow and find a quiet spot in the mountain to thrust my *pugio* into my heart.

She stopped when we reached a shaded avenue which led to the villa entrance and waved her servant away. She watched until the woman was out of earshot, then spun round to me and struck me in the face.

'That is for being a snotty Roman and treating me like a whore, but mostly for daring to insult my father. You are ignorant and uncultured. The sooner you crawl back to your village in rural Latium among the pigs and weaving women the better.'

'Why didn't you tell me who you were?'

'Why should I? I pick where I want.' Her eyes narrowed. 'And I decided you were what I wanted at that moment.'

'But I forced you.'

'Ha! You think I couldn't have disabled you? What a spoilt boy you are. Nevertheless, you performed well enough.'

'You're shameless. You behaved like a prostitute.'

'What, did you think you were the first?' Her voice was coated with contempt.

One foot in front of the other, hands raised, her eyes live as fire, she looked ready to start a fight. She drew her hand back, but I was ready for her. I grabbed both her wrists with one hand and circled her waist with my arm and pulled her in tight to stop her striking me again. Her body was warm and soft, and smelled of honey and a lingering aroma of something more elemental. I could have eaten her. I bent over her to kiss the base of her throat. She sighed. The next moment, my groin, hardening with desire, burst into agony as her knee drove into it.

'You little bitch,' I croaked, doubling over. I managed to hang on to one of her wrists and pulled her down with me. My body weight prevented her escaping, but she laughed at me as I took some quick breaths to recover. I grabbed her wrists over her head and eased her knees apart. Then she looked at me, the blue eyes unflinching.

'Do it, if you have any strength in your cock.'

Her legs curled up each side of my body. Her nipples showed hard against the silk of her robe as she arched her back. Her smile was pure invitation. Then she opened her lips.

'Are you well?' Opsius asked me as we walked back to the *castrum*. 'You haven't said a word. Were you dallying with the lovely Julia?'

'She certainly needs a strong hand,' I retorted.

'Was she that rude?' He laughed and slapped me on the back. 'Don't get burnt, she's known to be a firebrand. That's why she's living with her father again. She refuses to go back to her husband.' He shrugged. 'Mind you, despite his supposed patrician ancestors, that man's an idiot.'

I stopped and stared at him. 'Husband?'

'A nephew of the bishop. He always looks as if he's swallowed a jarful of unripe olives. Can you imagine it, the luscious Julia with a man who'd rather spend the evening praying than bedding her?' He made a mildly obscene gesture. 'That's why although the bishop's a bigwig round here neither he nor the nephew was at the dinner.'

Gods, what the hell was I getting into? Not only had I added adultery to my list of transgressions, but I'd stepped on the local religious leader's territory. My father was dismissive of the Galileans as charlatans with cannibalistic ceremonies; he was certain they'd fade away like any other crazy cult out of the East. I wasn't so sure. I disliked them for their lack of tolerance – there was no other reason why I'd been kicked out of Britannia – but my strategy was to keep out of their way. Well, that had worked.

'I'll give her this,' Opsius said. 'She walked out of the nephew's house one day, divorced him in the Celtic tradition and sent him a Roman writ of divorce as well – all in a day. The bishop says it's meaningless and that she's still married in the eyes of God. He's a crafty sod. Perhaps he saw her dowry slipping out of his family's control. Bacausus is as rich as Croesus, what with his metalworks and all his lands. Anyway, the nephew called on Bacausus, full of shit, demanding his wife, and I heard the prince told him to fuck off. Literally. Okay, I'll give the nephew credit for facing up to one of the *Palatini*, but the little sod was so full of crap about women's submission. Telling that to the Celts gets your ear chopped off around here, if you're not careful.'

I laughed. Submissive was the last word I'd use to describe Julia Bacausa.

'How do you know all that?' I asked.

'Are you that naive, Apulius?'

'Ah. You've got somebody in the prince's house.'

'Oh, well done. Not as thick as you look. Two somebodies, in fact.'

I grunted, and we walked on a few paces until we approached the *castrum* gate.

'Anyway,' he said, stopping out of the sentries' earshot, 'the following Sunday, the bishop ranted on about wifely duty for an hour, jabbing his finger at Julia. She looked up, stuck her tongue out at him in the middle of the church. The whole place went silent. She got up and stalked out, everybody watching. Uncle bishop and the prince are polite in public but have been locked in silent enmity ever since.'

Nobody was more surprised than I was to receive an invitation from her the next day to an open poetry reading at a friend's villa. Not one of my favourite pastimes, but she'd mocked me for being a peasant from Latium. Well, I'd dredge up some lines from my schooldays and show her.

On the front row of an audience of around fifty, Julia sat next to her father the whole evening, demure as a vestal in her white *stola* and *palla*, but her eyes flashed with enjoyment and she applauded sometimes politely, sometimes enthusiastically, after each poet finished. After an hour, a dark-haired man in his late thirties stood up at the back of the assembled guests and strutted to the front of the room. Julia frowned, then glanced at her father. He reached out and took her hand in both of hers. Several people glanced at them, then back to the poet. He bowed first to an older bearded man at the other end of the audience semicircle. With the Galilean cross on a chain round his neck, his rich robe and his confident air, this had to be the bishop. He smiled and nodded at the poet. Ah, Julia's husband or non-husband.

The nephew began his lines, pausing a little too dramatically. It was a pompous reflection on Roman domestic virtues. Julia's face became more and more rigid as he pointedly addressed his words in her direction. People in the audience started murmuring, but the poet ploughed on. After another minute, he stopped. The audience fell silent. He stretched his hand out to Julia and commanded, 'Come, wife. Now!'

Her skin flushed bright red. The prince was on his feet and stepped in front of her, facing the younger man.

'How dare you importune my daughter! She divorced you. Twice. That is final. Now leave this room while you still live.'

The prince's eyes bored into the face of the younger man, who took a step backwards. The bishop was by his side almost instantly.

'Now, prince, let us not quarrel in front of friends.'

'Keep out of this, Eligius,' Bacausus growled. 'Except you can take your young whelp home and keep him out of my sight.'

'Once he has his wife by his side, his companion under God, I'm sure that will be his pleasure.'

Bacausus turned to the bishop.

'I have no quarrel with you, Eligius, but I will not tolerate this kind of behaviour or the continuation of a private quarrel in public.'

The bishop merely smiled back, but said nothing.

The prince waited for a minute. The audience watched, mesmerised, as if this was another performance. Then Bacausus turned, took his daughter's hand and nodded to his host who stood along with many of the male guests including me. The caustic look he shot at the nephew should have destroyed the younger man on the spot and left only a small heap of ash. Bacausus made his way towards the door. But he found it blocked by two men with crossed staves.

'Out of my way,' he said in a voice that would have made even barbarians' stomachs turn liquid. One man flinched, the other looked down, then glanced at the bishop who gave a tiny shake of his head. I saw a smile on the bishop's face, mostly disguised by his beard. So, he'd set this up. Bastard.

I rested my hand on the grip of my grandfather's *gladius*, which I used as a dagger in town, and walked deliberately slowly towards the prince and his daughter. The guests parted like sheep. I'd put on my full uniform out of vanity; now it was a concrete sign for all the civilians that the power of the Roman army was in their midst.

'Allow me to escort you, prince,' I said. He narrowed his eyes. Julia's were wide.

'Thank you, tribune,' was all he said.

I stepped in front of him and gave the two men one of my best sneers. They hesitated for a second. Any longer, I'd have had them flogged.

'Will you stop pacing and sit down?' Bacausus growled at his daughter. 'You'll explode.'

'How dared he? How DARED he humiliate us like that?' Her red hair reflecting the flames of the torches, she was fizzing like an ancient Celtic goddess of fire.

'Julia, we have a guest. Come. Sit. Pour us some wine.'

'Wine? I want to throw it at that little prick.'

'Julia! Your mouth.'

She stopped. 'I apologise, Father. And to you, tribune.' She poured and mixed the drinks, handing me a cup with a tight smile.

'Well, that was a trap I hadn't foreseen,' Bacausus said. 'I am duly warned.' He raised his cup to me. 'My thanks, young man.'

'It was unconscionable, sir,' I said. 'A man supposed to be religious, playing a trick like that.'

'Unfortunately, a sign of changing times. Our power is fading. The Christians' is rising. When I fought with Julian, I hoped he'd redress the balance. But Fortuna intervened at Samarra.'

'Sir? I thought you worshipped with the Galileans – I mean, Christians.'

'Do I know you well enough to answer that?' he said, half to himself. 'It's politics, tribune,' he added in his normal voice. 'My people once ruled in Virunum by right before the Romans had ever heard of it. Now Noricum is divided into two Roman provinces and they allow me to rule in my little fiefdom. But they've planted this damn bishop here.' He waved his hand. 'Not exactly planted. Eligius's family come from Teurnia just up the valley, so he knows everything and everybody here. Julia and I go to his church once a week in order to keep the peace. It was working until his bloody nephew appeared on the scene.'

Julia had become quiet and was looking down at the mosaic floor, her eyes unfocused.

I desperately wanted to ask her why she'd married him, but I felt that was too intimate a question. Laughable, considering our previous encounters, but something had changed tonight. I'd seen her vulnerability, her anxiety under all that passion; it was a part of her inner nature that she'd kept buried.

As I left, she stood quietly in the vestibule beside her father. She brought her eyes up to mine.

'Thank you,' she whispered.

Bacausus invited me to eat with them whenever I wished, but I was strangely nervous. Julia herself became almost shy of me. She was the loveliest creature on earth, and I ached with wanting her, but I couldn't even touch her hand; it seemed so disrespectful now.

A week later, I invited her and her father to be my guests at the unit games. Opsius had felt as senior officer he was obliged to invite Bishop Eligius and, of course, the nephew, but I made sure we sat as far away as we could from them. We used one end of the old amphitheatre closed over fifty years ago for gladiatorial games. Constantine had been persuaded that the altars and reliefs dedicated to Nemesis and the sacred nature of the games were too pagan.

'If you look carefully you can still see the goddess's sanctuary at the eastern apex,' I whispered to Julia. 'Closed now, of course.'

'The old gods are important to you, aren't they, Lucius?' She searched my face, her own serious.

'I couldn't be a Roman without them.'

'But what does it mean to be Roman now?' She gestured at the men warming up with practice fights below in the sand, at the audience in a mixture of togas and ornate robes in the front rows, then at those sitting further back on the curved benches, mostly tribespeople in native dress and long hair.

I shrugged and looked back at the arena. Trumpets sounded, and the games began. Her eyes shone at the competitions, but she flinched when a young soldier was wounded.

'It's only a scratch,' I folded her hand in mine to reassure her.

'It could be you.'

'Would you care?' I held my breath for her answer.

She placed her other hand on top of mine and pressed it. 'Of course.'

I returned from patrol a week later and was handing a prisoner over to the interrogator when one of the prince's bodyguards approached me.

'Come. Now.'

Bacausus took me into his *tablinum*, his office at the back of the atrium, and pulled a screen across the opening.

'I've been watching you and my daughter.'

Gods. So this was the time to ask him for her hand. I drew myself up, ready, but he spoke before I could get one word out.

'She wants you, but the bishop won't budge. She confessed last night that she went to see him after the games. He says she would be committing spiritual adultery and condemning her eternal soul because you're a pagan as well as a foreigner.' He sighed. 'Much as I want to, I can't thrust his words back down his throat. I can't go against him – he's too powerful. I'm sorry.'

In one blow of his tongue, he'd felled me quicker than with a barbarian spear. That instant I realised how much I wanted Julia, not just in lust, but for love. As my life's companion.

'But what will happen to Julia? She can't return to that ghastly man.'

'No, she's divorced him legally. Roman law still runs here.'

'So just because she stood up with the nephew and muttered a few words in front of their priest, she is condemned to a half-life?'

'She didn't actually marry under the Christian rite. She followed the Celtic tradition. Her mother was a hillwoman, a German chief's daughter. I was with the legions and defeated the father for Rome and took the daughter for myself. A tough woman, but a precious one. She died when Julia was sixteen and made her daughter promise to marry in the tradition of the tribes. Julia insisted on honouring her dead mother. She made the Roman declaration in front of the governor afterwards, but she refused the Christian ceremony.' He sighed. 'Perhaps that was the first thing that soured the marriage.'

'But then Eligius and his Galileans have no hold over her,' I said. 'She and I can marry legally.'

'Oh, Eligius is a lot more subtle than that. He persisted she should be baptised, just to reassure his nephew who would be unhappy if his wife was technically a pagan. She eventually gave in for the nephew's sake – I think she saw it was creating problems in the marriage – and he now says she's a Christian wife.'

'But that's ridiculous!'

'Yes, of course it is, but he's got the church behind him and he has powerful friends in Rome, even access to the emperor, they say.'

'Gods.'

'I'm sorry, Lucius. She fell for a handsome face and polished manners. She bitterly regrets it, but feels tied.' He looked away for a moment, then brought his gaze back to me. 'You should go now.'

'I can't. I must see Julia first.'

'No. That would just stir her up and I won't have her more upset than she is already.' He stood and opened the screen across the *tablinum* entrance. 'Go with dignity, Lucius Apulius, or be thrown into the street like a beggar.'

I had never seen such a hard expression in his eyes.

That night, I got drunk. So drunk I had to be revived by the *medicus* and spent the next two days shivering and boiling alternately in my bed. And then the letter arrived from Rome – my commission in the Roman army was terminated with immediate effect.

Rome

Back in Rome, my father, the so-called pagan, had held his own. The city still needed fresh food and wine and our estate in Latium produced good quantities of both. He kicked me out of the city house for being moody and sent me into the country. I found the hard routine of managing and working on the farm left me no time for self-pity, but I ached for the loss of Julia. I'd had no letter from her. She could read and write Latin and Greek perfectly well, she'd stated tartly when I'd asked her. I itched to travel to Virunum and just fetch her, but I was forbidden to go beyond Latium.

I was screwing my eyes up, checking the list of the latest consignment of fruit and vegetables to go to our market stalls in the city, when Zolcius, our overseer, asked for permission for a day off.

'My daughter's getting married, sir, to one of these Christians.' He didn't look very happy about it. 'She has to take a ritual bath, or something, beforehand or she can't marry the boy. Apparently, once that's done, she could marry any of them.'

I dropped my stylus and felt my jaw slacken.

'You can have the whole week off, Zolcius. Just get my horse saddled first.'

'It's a rejection of so much I hold dear,' I said to my father when I sought his permission that evening to convert. 'I belong to Mars and always will. I will honour the gods every day in my heart until the day I die. But I shall go mad if I have to endure life without Julia.'

His stricken face nearly stopped me. 'You would give up so much for this woman?'

'Yes.'

'It's your choice, Lucius. Undoubtedly, your everyday life will become easier as a Christian; you may be able to take up soldiering again, but beware of a canker growing in your mind and soul.'

I bowed my head, feeling his sadness and mine. That night as we sacrificed to Mars and Jupiter, my father intoned prayers of mourning. I whispered an additional one to Mercury, patron of liars.

The next day, I bathed then dressed in my best toga. The nearest Christian church was only a few streets away. As I trudged from the atrium towards the street door, I nodded to our porter. He stepped forward, face eager to say something.

'I'm sorry to bother your honour, but that woman's here again. I told the steward and he said to send her off. A foreigner, but she looks respectable, with a maid and all.'

'Well, do what the steward says,' I replied and gestured him to open the door. As I stepped through I looked back and said to him. 'I can't delay. I have an important meeting.'

'And what, pray, is more important than meeting me?'

I caught my breath and whipped round.

The voice, the blue eyes and red hair. Julia. She smiled. I stared at her, my mouth open.

'I've been travelling for nearly four weeks by litter, ship and mule. I'm parched. You could at least ask me in. And then you can marry me, Lucius, according to your gods.'

AD 395

The Altar of Victory served as the pagan symbol of Rome's endurance, the guarantor of the empire's existence. But as the official imperial cult of Christianity swept all before it, Victory's fate was condemned to historical obscurity.

However, in the Roma Novan timeline, Victory herself tells us the story of how two senators and a small child step in.

VICTORY SPEAKS

If you've read PERFIDITAS you may remember when Carina went to speak in the Senate in her disguised character. But she was unaware that she was being watched...

The young woman shot a quick glance at me as she entered the Senate House that day, but I saw the over-lively eyes, the too much spring in her step, her chin ahead of the rest of her. Her hair was curled and black instead of the red-gold waves that belonged to her. She wore black clothes and over the top a traditional long white *palla* drawn up over her head in a semblance of modesty. Better than the sand-coloured breeches and shirt she usually wore like her fellow soldiers. Today another woman attended her, and two mercenaries in black with grim faces. She made her offering; a pinch of incense between hurrying hands and a few words of prayer for victory.

But I knew her despite her disguise. She was linked by blood to those other daring souls who had saved me over fifteen hundred years ago from the Galilean destroyers.

Fresh from his victory at the Frigidus River, four hundred years after their god was born, Theodosius the Christian strode into the Senate, paused and stared at me with his hard fanatic's eyes. I did not tremble: I was made of gold and full of power.

When the Romans seized me six centuries before, when Pyrrhus of

Epirus abandoned me in Tarentum, I ceased being Nike, who had fought alongside the Olympian gods against the Titans, and became Victory. Octavian brought me to his city after defeating the Egyptian queen and her lover. When he recast himself as Augustus, he placed me in the Senate and recast me as the symbol of Rome, her *numen*. While I stood, Rome would never fall.

But now twenty of Theodosius's soldiers marched into the *curia*, ignoring the shocked faces of the senators. Chattering like chickens, they fell silent when the centurion gave a curt command to the work party to approach the ancient square altar.

I soared over it, golden, wings outstretched, one leg forward escaping the wind-caught robe, my feet barely touching the marble. My arm, bent at a shallow angle at the elbow, offered the laurel crown to the victor. In my other hand, I grasped a palm branch, the tip resting on my shoulder. I was the guarantor of Rome's power.

Now they were destroying it – and me.

The legionaries surrounded me in silence, hesitating. A trace of incense hung in the air, but through it I could smell the soldiers' fear. They glanced at the watching senators, the walls, the floor, each other, but none dared to look up at me. If I could have taken flight, I would have scattered them like panicking sheep.

When their commander barked at them to get on with it, they grasped my legs and skirts with their nervous hands and lifted me off.

'No!'

A tall man in his upper forties, Lucius Apulius, a senator from an old family, darted towards the door to block the impious soldiers. The centurion drew his sword and thrust it in Apulius's face. The senator didn't flinch, but an arm as inflexible as iron barred him going further. His father.

'Sheathe your sword, centurion,' Apulius senior commanded. 'You are within the Senate precincts.'

The soldier snorted. 'Begging your honour's pardon,' he said, 'but that don't mean much these days. I take my orders from the legate who takes them direct from the emperor. Stand aside.'

Neither of the Apulii moved. The legionaries shuffled round them, sweating as they pulled a builder's handcart up the steps and hefted the altar into it like a piece of building stone. Two came back, turned me on my face as if I'd dived to my death, and manhandled me out through the door onto a second cart.

It was past midnight in the imperial contractor's yard. From the back of the workshop I heard a horse whinny. A man gasped. Another hushed him.

The first whispered, 'Jupiter, if that watchman or some bastard of a patrol comes this way, we're ash in the sacred flame.'

An empty threat – the vestals' holy flame had been extinguished after a thousand years. Theodosius's men had already expelled Coelia Concordia, the last *vestalis maxima*, from the holy College of Vestals and sealed the temple door.

The sound of a key in a lock, the creak of a door. Two men crept in, letting the moonlight slip in for a second. Door closed, one struck a fire steel and lit a taper, a thin, poor thing like a military field torch. The smoky, flickering light was enough to throw up shadows of lifting braces, hammers, chisels, saws and axes, and half the face of Apulius's friend, Mitelus.

He wove his way through the jumble of half-worked stone, parts of columns, and a chipped statue with one arm. Struggling towards the back, he tripped over one of the large wedges used for splitting stone. He threw his hand out and found my wing.

'Jupiter!' He steadied himself, coughing with the dust. 'Apulius. Here.'

They swaddled me in rough sacking and their cloaks and carried me across the yard, past open-ended bins with sand, small stones and loose materials, the lean-tos down one side with blocks of stone, marble, red curved tiles piled up. They set me down carefully. The yard gate creaked, then thudded as it closed. But we hadn't moved.

'Where the Hades is this driver of yours?' Gaius Mitelus's voice was strong but anxious. 'Can we trust him?'

'Nobody better,' Apulius answered.

'Everybody's trustworthy until they get paid enough or it's beaten out of them.'

'I'd put my life in Titus Calavius's hands.'

'You may well have done tonight.'

'For Mars' sake, Gaius, he served with me up on the Danube, then Noricum. Despite his loyal service, he was passed over several times because he wouldn't fully embrace the Galilean way. Believe me, if he said he'll be here, he'll be here.'

The sound of wheels on the street stopped their bickering. A horse snickered.

The gate creaked again but longer, and they carried me out and laid me on foul-smelling boards.

'*Merda*, I thought you'd got caught,' Apulius said as he climbed up. He sniffed. 'Speaking of shit, where the hell did you get this wagon?'

'Ha! It's the one the stable uses for shovelling dung,' a new voice said. 'Good disguise, no? Nobody will want to inspect it.'

Apulius laughed.

'Go!' Mitelus smacked the horse's rump and leapt on the back as the wagon started moving.

The Greek's studio was not far. When they pulled the sacking and cloaks away from me, his eyes widened, but almost immediately, he started measuring me, assessing every fold and curve.

'Ten days,' he said at last to Apulius and Mitelus. They nodded, handed over a purse then bowed to me.

The Greek worked, tapping and chipping behind a screen. Small pieces of stone plinked onto the flagstones. A curse erupted now and then. I smiled to myself. Despite my centuries with the Latin-speakers, my head was still Greek. He darted back and forth looking at me, sometimes making little sketches, then back to his chipping and tapping.

I smelled glue boiling, the sound of beating then grinding metal and brushstrokes, lapping and dabbing. On the tenth day came the heavy footsteps of two men entering the studio. They grunted with the strain of lifting something. An obscenity. I heard a cackle of laughter from the Greek. I glimpsed a wing tip, a similar shape to mine, but crudely carved and painted dull gold, moving above the screen. Then it disappeared.

Apulius and Mitelus returned the following day. Apulius bowed to me and said, 'Forgive us for what we must do. It is only to save you.' He gestured to Mitelus, who placed a pot in front of me, dipped a brush in it and covered me in grey paint. Before it could dry, Apulius showered me with chalk powder and fine grit. Then another coat of paint, then grey sand and lime. They didn't hear my growls as they obliterated my gold, my fine feathering, the sheen of my robe. Mitelus stayed in the Greek's studio that night, bedded down on a mattress with his sword inches from his hand.

His friend returned the next day in the afternoon, their fingers touching and dabbing at me. Apparently satisfied, they wrapped me in cloths. Coins clinked as if from one hand to another — a good number of them — then a murmured 'Go with the gods,' in Greek.

I stood for weeks in Apulius's garden, just another dull statue, covered some days in frost, others in rain and growing a thin coat of moss.

A month later, a girl, twelve or thirteen years old, red-gold curls running all over her head and down her back, pelted along the garden path. She stopped in front of me. She glanced backward, then jumped into the shrubs behind me and crouched down, leaning against my plinth. A young woman, darker, hurried down the path.

'Julia Apulia,' she called out. 'If you don't come out *now* from where you're hiding, you're going to get such a whipping my arm will ache.'

I felt the young one tremble.

'Galla?' A man's voice. Apulius.

'Father.' She dropped her eyes for a second, but raised them almost immediately. 'It's Julia. She's run off again.'

'Darling, I don't think she's the type to sit indoors on a sunny day, learning her letters or sewing cloth.'

'How can you be so tolerant? She's immodest, unruly—'

'And full of spirit,' he finished, his mouth smiling, but his eyes bleak. Perhaps he remembered his dead wife, the first Julia, the tough daughter of the Celtic princeling Bacausus. He'd stood one evening in front of me nearly weeping as he told me his story. His Julia had left her native Noricum, pursued the young tribune as he was then to Rome and married him. Revelling in her three daughters, she'd known her Roman husband needed a son. But having tried for the fourth time, she'd gone into the shades the night little Julia was born.

Apulius smiled now at his serious eldest daughter and took her hand. 'Peace, Galla. We have so little time here.'

When the buds on the roses started to split, two servants came and wrapped me in sacking, folding rough cloth round my wings, my head, the delicate palm I carried. They padded my whole figure with wadding and laid me in a freshly made pinewood box.

We travelled in wagons for several weeks. From the myriad voices – men, women and children – the time we took to cross bridges, the shouts and horses galloping, I calculated several hundred souls were travelling with us. Little Julia rode in my wagon, sitting or lying on a pile of blankets and cushions, her hand resting on my box, sometimes telling me stories about her past and possible future, about the twelve families travelling with us, the squabbling and the sharing on the journey north. Sometimes I heard soft, rhythmic breathing when, despite the jolting wagon, she'd fallen asleep. At dusk, when we stopped, one of her sisters would fetch the exhausted child to her pallet in their tent.

Only once did I hear shouting, the clashing of weapons, a violent thump against my wagon which made it rock. Two hands thrust a bundle in a blanket through the leather flap at the back in the dark of the night. I recognised the voices immediately – Julia and Galla.

'Stay hidden, behind the wooden crate,' Galla said in an urgent whisper which I just heard above the cries and noise of fighting. 'You must stay as still as Victory until I fetch you.'

'Don't leave me, Galla,' Julia pleaded.

'Victory will protect you. I must go and fight.'

Clashes of metal on metal, women's and men's shouting. Eventually, the noise faded. Galla returned just before dawn, her face dirty and a smear of blood on her face. Julia was fast asleep, her arm across my box and her face peaceful. We had protected each other.

One evening when we halted, I heard a heavy bolt drawn back and the rattle of a gate opening to let us pass through. Leather creaked as they unfastened the traces and lifted the yokes to release the mules. The noises faded. I was alone for the first time in two months.

The next day, two men unpacked me and set me on a low pedestal in between two yew trees overlooking a wide river valley. The air was fresher – mixed with woodsmoke and animals. I smelled olives and pine resin and saw mountains, not the scraped dry crusts of

Hellas, but lush, green meadows full of delicate purple and yellow flowers.

Julia brought a tall grey-haired man to see me. Bearded, and wearing a thick gold torc around his neck, he was no Roman. Her soft, almost babyish hand nestled in the big man's paw.

'Grandfather, this is my friend. Everybody calls her Victory, but in her head she's Nike. She keeps us safe.'

They built their town, Roma Nova, crude at first, only a *decumanus maximus* crossed by a *cardo max*, but it grew. They bred warrior sons and daughters who defended their valley from would-be invaders. Mitelus died in battle six years after arriving; his friend Apulius, their leader, their *imperator*, was stricken by wounds. Apulius's daughters, Galla, Lucilla, Claudia and not so little Julia, prayed in front of me, their faces strained, their bodies clad in chain shirts and leather breeches, swords at their waists. Like their mother's family and hers before her, they went into battle with their male cousins and friends against invading barbarians. They won, but at great cost.

When Julia Apulia was a grandmother of fifty with white and grey hair interwoven with fading red, she came to me in the garden. She limped and leaned heavily on a stick. Clutching her free hand was a girl, about eleven or twelve years old, with Julia's red hair but darker, brown with copper burnt too long.

Julia bowed to me, slowly and stiffly.

'This is my dead son's child, Cloelia Mitela, also the granddaughter of Gaius Mitelus who helped rescue you all those years ago.' Julia raised her eyes up to mine. 'I hope you will be her friend like you have been mine.' She closed her eyes for a moment. Her face sagged and I saw how old she looked, well beyond her natural age, from a hard life and many battles.

She beckoned forward two men and an overgrown adolescent carrying cloths, buckets and builders' tools.

'This is Victory,' Julia said to them, 'our spirit, our guardian. You are to clean her with the utmost care until she shines through.'

The men exchanged glances for several seconds, then laid cloths around my base, picked up their tools and started chipping at the grey crust. The boy climbed onto a stool, raised his small hammer and sculptor's chisel. With his first tap on the concrete coating, he shattered my wing.

Julia blenched and swayed. Cloelia wrapped her arms around her grandmother's waist and cried out, 'Nonna!'

'Get that oaf a hundred miles from me,' Julia hissed.

One workman bundled the boy away. Cloelia bent down and gently picked up the shattered gold and cement feathers. She instructed the other workman to take me to the master smith and walked by the cart to his studio, supporting the furious Julia and speaking soft words to her.

When the smith shook his head, Cloelia insisted he attempt the repair. She came every day with Julia, watching gravely as they tried and failed four times. They hadn't rediscovered the gold seams mined and abandoned by their forebears, so they had no gold to use. Reluctantly, but not daring to cross Julia, the smith used precious silver clawed out of the new mine. The fifth attempt was clumsy, but he succeeded. A sorry state of affairs, but the new colony had sacrificed its tiny wealth for me.

The day before my final journey, Cloelia came alone. 'Nonna can't come today. She's sick and has to stay in bed.' Her shoulders drooped, but she managed to smile up at me. 'I'll come and see you tomorrow when you're in the new Senate House.'

Tall, polished stone walls rose to double height, topped with a red tile roof. Columns at each corner supported the covered public forecourt rising from wide steps at the formal entrance. Dominating the inner hall stood a new square pedestal, polished and gleaming, widening out at the top with a shallow dip carved out for offerings. Two women and two men lifted me onto the altar. I soared over the people who had saved me. I swore I would protect them to the last ounce of my power, until the end of days.

Imperatrix Galla and her two sisters, Lucilla and Claudia, their daughters and sons, members of the Twelve Families who as children had made the long trek to found Roma Nova, stood in silence before me. The priestess poured a libation, dropped a pinch of incense and intoned ritual prayers.

After the adults left, Cloelia laid myrtle leaves at the foot of the altar.

'Nonna couldn't be here to see you in your proper place.' Her face glistened with tears. 'She crossed the Styx last night, but before she went, she begged Great Aunt Galla not to stop your rededication. She said it was her life's dream.'

She bowed her dark copper head, wiped her hand across her eyes, turned and escaped through the public forecourt. She stumbled down the steps into her mother's arms.

As the sun set, another slight figure with translucent red-gold curls that didn't reflect the dusk light, came and settled by the altar. Gone were the mature lines, the grey hair, the battle-scarred arms of her older self. Now the young girl as she had been when she'd first befriended me decades ago had returned to sit with me. She almost merged into the stone. She looked up and smiled. I smiled down.

She was still sitting with me the day a millennium and a half later when we watched her descendant enter the Senate House to fight her own battle.

1066

Galla Mitela, eleventh century imperial councillor, is sent by the imperatrix under pressure from the Eastern Romans of Constantinople to stop William of Normandy invading Saxon England.

Could she have succeeded?

(Previously published as part of the 1066 Turned Upside Down *collection)*

A ROMAN INTERVENES

'Gods, Galla, how long are we going to be stuck in this cursed boat?'

I stood in the prow and looked down at my cousin huddling in her misery. She'd puked all the way across the British Sea to Gaul and almost all the way down the Sequana River that the Normans called the Seine. Poor child. Claudia was only seventeen and hated going out on the river at home.

'Not long now. The shipmaster assures me we'll reach Rotomagus this afternoon.' No, Rou-en. Gods, it sounded like a donkey braying.

It was only the fourth day since we'd left the harbour near Magnus Portus, now the Saxon port of Bosham. We'd headed across the choppy water for Bononia. Once known as Gesoriacum and, until that pirate emperor Carausius seized it, the proud home of the Roman *Classis Britannica*, the fleet supplying the vital link between Gaul and Britannia.

As we'd sailed past, it looked like a scruffy little hole in the wall, its dock silted up and the one remaining harbour wall half derelict. Well, its function as northern fleet headquarters had been over six centuries ago. What had I expected? Little had been built, let alone maintained, since our ancestors left Gaul.

We'd sailed further south down the coast, passing the wide bay of the Samara. The salt tang of the open sea was invaded by the smell of brackish marshes. Screwing my eyes up and peering across the wide, open expanse of the flatlands, I'd seen a group of tiny warships bobbing in the water in the natural harbour. They were making their way towards us, the harbour mouth and ultimately the open sea. But we passed by before they came anywhere near us.

I shivered in the chill of the early morning and drew my cloak around me. Instead of the pale breaking light of a clear sky heralding a fair summer's day, it was misty and overcast again. Our Saxon escort from the ship *fyrd*, their fleet, left us, setting off for the safety of England before we entered the mouth of the Sequana. We sailed past a boatyard on the south bank, too frantic with activity even at that hour to notice another foreign trading ship. Tents and ramshackle huts clustered around a village the shipmaster called Hunefloth. I could hear the clanging of metal upon metal across the open water.

We sailed upriver only passing the occasional small vessel dwarfed by our trader; the land either side was mostly wooded but interspersed with fields and peasants' cottages. No farms or villas, just the occasional jetty or mooring point. As we rounded the steep headland dominated by the castle of Robert the Devil, I wondered what kind of reception we would get at Rotomagus.

We'd left the Saxon port with many good wishes for our travels, food and wine for our journey and a sad smile from one particular warrior on the quayside. Eadmær. I grasped the wooden rail harder. I'd watched until his tall figure had diminished to a blur. If we failed, I would never see him again. If we succeeded, he was his king's man and would never come back with me to Roma Nova. I released my breath.

'Still dreaming of your yellow-haired Saxon?' Claudia gave me a knowing look. 'Is he blond all over his body?'

I felt the warmth crawling up my neck into my face. 'No concern of yours, child. Be silent.' I frowned at her.

'I'm not a child and you can't talk to me in that way. You might be the senior countess and my mother's chief advisor, but I'm her daughter and heir!'

'Then behave like it. The imperatrix would be ashamed of your behaviour.'

She shrugged and turned her back to me and pretended to study the scenery. She sulked until we rounded the last bend in the Sequana and saw our destination. A small town on a flat river plain, based on the earlier walled *castrum*, squatted against wooded hills. As we approached the mooring point to the west, away from the shallow channels and low islands, we could see work parties labouring to build a more formal quayside. On deck, our servants busied themselves preparing our bundles for disembarkation to smaller boats which would take us to the solid ground of the town. Claudia leaned towards me.

'Aren't we going to change?'

'There's nothing wrong with how we are dressed,' I replied. 'We are as we are.' Our wool tunics over linen shirts, trousers, long boots and wool hooded cloaks were practical for travelling. Both of us had tied our hair back in a single long plait, although Claudia's curly brown hair sprang away and framed her face. And we'd taken the precaution of wearing our imperial badges.

'*Domina.*' The Praetorian centurion nodded his head in the direction of a small boat coming towards us. I leaned over the side and watched as two men scrambled up the rope ladder one of our sailors had let down.

The first over the rail was a dark-haired, close-shaven sturdy man who had little trouble heaving himself on board. He was followed by a slighter man who had hitched his long tunic up into his belt to scale the side and fidgeted as he smoothed it back down. His head was shaved on the crown; a priest. The first man, dressed in a maroon tunic with embroidered edging and a silver belt, cast around, passed over Claudia and me and addressed himself to the centurion.

'I am Gilbert de Boscville,' he said, to the centurion. 'Where is your commander?' He spoke in Latin with an accent so thick I could barely understand.

The Saxons had warned us about de Boscville; he was one of Duke William's close aides, a harsh ruler of his lands and fiercely loyal to his master. I nodded to the centurion, who drew back.

'I am Galla Mitela, imperial councillor and Countess of the South, leading the Roma Nova delegation,' I began. 'May I present Claudia Apulia, daughter and heir of Imperatrix—'

'Where is the commander?' he interrupted and waved impatiently.

The servants froze. Some gasped. The centurion drew his sword and closed the gap between Claudia and de Boscville. The remaining Praetorians took a step closer to me.

De Boscville frowned, but stepped back at the centurion's fierce glare.

'My Lord de Boscville, you are insolent as well as ignorant,' I said in my coldest voice. 'Have the goodness to wait until I have finished speaking. And listen to each word carefully.'

Claudia stared at me. Perhaps she had never heard me reprimand anybody so severely.

De Boscville flushed and the features on his dark face drew closer.

'I do not deal with *women*. Where is the senior man? I am to escort him and his delegation to my lord duke.'

'Then you are destined to be disappointed. He does not exist.' I flicked my hand impatiently. 'Are we to remain here all night waiting on your dignity? If Duke William does not wish to hear the latest news from England, then we will set sail now.' I turned and waved to the shipmaster. 'Plot a course downriver away from this barbarian place and find us a berth for the night. Tomorrow we return to Roma Nova.'

'At once, *domina*.' He bowed and hurried off, waving his arm and shouting orders at the crew.

'The Praetorians will see you off my ship, Lord de Boscville, or you will be sailing with us.' I turned my back on him and grasped Claudia's arm.

'What are you doing?' she hissed at me as we entered the little cabin amidships.

'Tactics, my girl. You wait and see.'

'But Mother will kill you if you don't see the duke. She says you have to stop this war.'

'We'll see him, don't worry.' I smiled to myself and counted the heartbeats that passed.

Five minutes later, we were climbing down the rope ladder to the small boat waiting below. We'd declined the sling usually used for 'ladies'. De Boscville scowled in silence, forced to have acknowledged us. To be truthful, he looked ill. As the boat bobbed in the water, I smiled graciously at the priest who promptly crossed himself, no doubt warding himself against the pagan Romans. On the riverside, a troop of horsemen were waiting for us with spare mounts. Their captain looked at de Boscville, a question on his face.

'You can ride, I assume?' he said.

I said nothing, but Claudia and I swung up onto the two tallest horses in reply. The six Praetorians were given mounts and fell in behind us, immediately in front of de Boscville's men. Our servants would follow on mules with the baggage.

'Pray lead on, my lord,' I said in my most condescending tone and nodded. He grunted and led off.

'Well, it's comfortable enough, but not warm,' Claudia said. She fidgeted on a velvet-covered padded stool as my body servant teased her curly hair up into an intricate pattern of plaits holding her diadem secure. I pressed my hand onto her shoulder.

'Sit still, child, and let Marcia do her work.' I draped her wool *stola* across her shoulders. 'We have to look as imposing as possible. The duke is a hard man, but apparently impressed by ceremony. That is why you must wear gold in your hair and purple on your back.'

'But I don't understand why you are wearing your Praetorian *lorica*.' She ran her eye down my figure. Like hers, my hair was bound up in classic Roman style, but plainer. Over a dark green tunic which nearly reached the floor but didn't cover my senator's red boots, I wore Praetorian *lorica hamata*, the chain mail shirt complete with *phalerae* I'd earned. I'd tied a simple black knotted legionary's *focale* around my neck against the draughts. Hung across my shoulders was the silver chain collar with the Mitela badge decorated with enamelled myrtle leaves and miniature eagles. And whatever de Boscville had said about bearing arms in the castle, my *gladius* was firmly attached at the left to my gold and leather belt along with a ceremonial *pugio* dagger on the right. The combined weight was not inconsiderable. I'd chosen a dark green cloak pinned with a chased gold fibula my mother had given me when I became an imperial councillor. I touched it for luck. May her spirit and Juno guide me tonight.

A knock on the door interrupted my thoughts and my answer to Claudia. The Praetorian commander and his troop waited in formation in the corridor. The flickering torches in the wall sconces reflected on their polished helmets. I held my hand out to Claudia.

'Come, *principissa*.'

'Don't call me by that stupid name, Galla. That's what *he* calls me.' Her face flushed red with anger. I pressed her fingers in sympathy and kept my own sourness inside. 'He', or as I called him in my head 'that Eastern bastard', was Claudia's mother's current companion, Gregory.

He'd arrived two years ago from Constantinople, a natural son of the late emperor Constantine Monomachos, and had spent that time worming his way into the imperatrix's favour. He was behind me being sent on this mission, cozening the imperatrix, saying I was equipped with unique statecraft gifts and experience to mediate between Saxons and Northmen. As her chief advisor, I was obviously in his way in his quest for power. Roma Nova had been pressured by the Eastern Roman emperor to mediate between Normandy and England: the Saxons were valuable trading partners for them as well as for Roma Nova. Although many Norman mercenaries served the Eastern Empire's military forces, the emperor was wary of their expansion into Italy. The Norman warriors were fierce, efficient and usually victorious. Nothing seemed to stop them; perhaps it was the wolfish Viking blood that ran in their veins. If Normandy won England and dominated the North their power would increase considerably.

Unfortunately, Gregory had been present when the imperatrix had received the messenger from Constantinople. Lost in the joys of forthcoming late motherhood, she had nodded her head to his suggestion and I was dispatched. I was caught for now by the imperatrix's command, but when I returned, things would change.

'I apologise, *domina*,' I said, and bowed to her daughter in front of me. Claudia frowned, then broke into a wide smile. Now engulfed in her purple wool *stola*, she would feel the chill from the stone walls less. But her sandalled feet must have frozen on the stone slabs. She grasped my hand, straightened her back and we set off.

The ducal palace built by Duke William's father was imposing; the stone tower dominated but as we were shown into the *Aula Turris*, the *Grande Salle*, I was struck not only by the heat but also by the sheer luxury of its proportions and decoration. Here ruled a man of power indeed. At the top of the walls ran a blind arcade of semi-circular arches under which were hangings of rich reds, blues and greens, some embroidered with gold and silver thread. But even richer were the gowns and jewelled belts of the women in the hall and the tunics and mantles of their men.

At the far end on a raised dais were William and Matilda. A slim figure, the duchess's eyes were full of curiosity. Like the other women present her hair was hidden beneath a veil, hers below a gold circlet, but of such softness it could only have been the sheer silk from Constantinople. But William was the opposite of the delicate elegance of his wife. From the heavy gold circle with a large cabochon ruby shining from its centre on his head, down the dark crimson robe and over-mantle clothing his sturdy frame, belted by gold, down to his dark boots, he exuded wealth and strength. His eyes fixed on us from the moment we stood on the threshold of the hall until we reached the two thrones where they sat.

'*Salvete dux ducissaque,*' I began. William frowned, but Matilda smiled although she said nothing. De Boscville stepped out of the lines of courtiers, his face creased in irritation. He translated my greeting into French, then turned and said in Latin, 'Continue.'

'Forgive me, Duke William,' I said in French. I paused and smiled. 'I had not realised you did not speak Latin.'

William frowned again and shot a hard look at me. I knew perfectly well he couldn't even read or write his own native tongue.

'I present Claudia Apulia,' I said. 'She brings greeting from her mother, the imperatrix of Roma Nova.'

He nodded curtly and stared her up and down like a piece of meat. She flushed slightly, but looked back steadily at him. Matilda laid her fingers on his forearm.

'We have been asked to convey a message to you from Harold the Saxon king.'

'The only message I want from the *earl* is the surrender of my rightful crown.'

'That, Duke William, is not for negotiation.' Some of the courtiers present murmured, and one man, another priest who I thought must be Lanfranc, his Galilean councillor, bent and whispered in the duke's ear. I waited until the murmuring had stopped and I had their attention again. 'Harold does not wish for warfare, but as you know from his campaign against the Welsh, he will not hesitate to enter the field in force if England is threatened. He proposes a treaty, starting with a calming period over the winter.'

'He is forsworn. That is an end on it. You are women but even you as Romans understand an oath is an oath.'

'Of course, but some would say he swore under duress.'

'You push too hard, woman.'

'I merely state the obvious, Duke.'

'We will think about it.'

'All the while you are mustering your invasion fleet?'

The murmuring rose to a clamour. Somebody muttered, 'Godless bitches.' Claudia took a sharp breath in at that but we stood still and waited.

'Peace!' the duke's voice rang out. 'The countess and princess are our guests. We will eat.' He stood and beckoned me to accompany him. Matilda smiled at Claudia, took her arm and followed us, the courtiers trailing in our wake.

A hard, uncompromising man with few social manners but willing to talk of common interests, he was deeply interested in how Roma Nova had been founded and in my own early career, sword in hand. I think he almost forgot I was a woman as we discussed campaigns and tactics. His eyes gleamed when I showed him the intricately worked *pugio* dagger. His acquisitiveness wasn't merely for a crown.

'Please accept it as a gift, Duke,' I said. 'Whatever happens in the future, it will be a souvenir of the Romans who once visited you.'

'I accept, most willingly.' He gave a half-smile. 'But you will not cozen me with your words and gifts.'

'I regret we cannot convince you of a peaceful way. I urge you to reconsider the advantages of a treaty. It will bring you more security in the end.'

'As your people have found.' He gave me a sardonic look. 'But you are now at the beck and call of the Greeks in the East.'

I bit my lip. 'Only for the moment, Duke. Sometimes, we have to endure discomfort for the sake of peace. The Eastern Romans have many troubles and have lost the earlier resolution of the times of Constantine. Roma Nova may yet outlive them.'

'Ha!' He searched my face while a servant refilled my cup. 'You are a strong woman, Countess, but why are you here? Should you not be tending your family?'

'I am the imperatrix's chief councillor, Duke. My children are grown and my life is given to the service of my ruler.'

I dismissed the body servants and combed Claudia's hair out myself. I needed to move my shoulders and arms after shedding the weight of my *lorica*.

'Did Matilda say anything interesting to you?'

'She is devoted to the duke, she busies herself with her children, their contracted marriages, her devotion to the Galilean god, her temple-building projects.' Claudia twisted round. 'She has a lively mind and sees everything, but although rich and admired, she has no purpose beyond that. I think she frets about the duke and his obsession with England. But she is a conventional wife and will not question his actions.'

'So, we cannot influence him via that route.' I stopped and laid my hands on Claudia's shoulders. She looked into the polished surface of her mirror.

'Did Mama give you any other orders?'

'Yes, but they may put us in danger.'

'But we must still follow them.'

'Yes. You are growing up too fast, Claudia Apulia.'

'No faster than any of our ancestors, Galla.'

Duke William was occupied inspecting an important building today, de Boscville announced to me as we broke bread the next morning. I glanced at him, but his harsh features revealed nothing. I suspected the 'building' under inspection would be naval rather than stone. The duchess had invited us to sit with her and the other women until the evening when his master would give me his formal answer.

'Claudia Apulia would be delighted to accept,' I said, ignoring Claudia's look of surprise swiftly followed by one of annoyance. 'However, I would, with Duchess Matilda's permission, like to visit Iuliobona – Lillebonne.'

'Why?'

'Pure sentiment. One of my ancestors was stationed there as a tribune and wrote an account of his time. It was an important and wealthy regional centre as well as a port to Britannia. I should like to see the remains. I believe the theatre was a fine one which could seat three thousand.' I smiled at him, but he frowned back. He was the surliest man I had ever met.

We jogged along the dirt road on good strong mounts, de Boscville and I, followed by two Praetorians and two of his men-at-arms. He'd insisted on accompanying me; I didn't know whether as guard or escort. It would be his misfortune if he became weary inspecting the relics of past times that meant nothing to him. His ancestors were probably scratching around northern mountains eating raw fish they'd caught that morning, or hunched in smelly huts round an open fire while mine ruled the known world.

After a midday meal in a tavern where de Boscville's autocratic manner secured us a table and good if terrified service, I asked to see the commercial part of the town. I smiled when I saw the main street of shops and stalls was called the Rue des Césars, presumably the Decumanus Maximus of old Iuliobona. I was looking for a cloth merchant; the wool was fine here and would make a suitable gift for the imperatrix. But that wasn't the only reason I stopped in front of one timber-framed building.

Inside, the merchant showed us bolts of both fine and sturdy cloth dyed in a variety of colours.

'We have colleagues from England, my lady, with some of their special South Downs wool cloth that's both warm and light.' He ushered me towards the far side of his hall where a young man stood folding a length of rich copper cloth. Darker than red ochre, yet hinting at burnt gold, the cloth was so supple it seemed almost alive. It would be a pity to hand it to the imperatrix as she would probably give it to Gregory.

Behind the table, his blond-haired companion sat on a folding stool and bent over a wax tablet on which he was making marks in a column; it looked like a tally. He looked up at my approach.

Eadmær.

He stared hard at me, almost frowning. I didn't say his name aloud, but my heart thudded. What in the depths of Tartarus was *he* doing here, right under the nose of William's people and obviously in disguise?

I glanced at de Boscville who sat at the side, drinking the merchant's ale, tapping his fingers on his thigh as I made my choices. I fingered some of the cloth as if considering purchasing it but couldn't stop looking at Eadmær. I lowered my voice and asked the merchant for the privy. His wife led me down a narrow passageway to the back door giving onto the courtyard.

I slumped against the back of the building to catch my breath for a moment and steady my heart. I thought Eadmær safe in England. If de Boscville even suspected one of Harold's most faithful aides was only a few steps away... As I turned in the direction the merchant's wife had indicated, hands grabbed me and pulled me behind the privy hut.

'I thought you would never arrive,' Eadmær whispered.

'What in Hades are you doing here?' I hissed back.

He grinned at me. 'I put myself forward to lead the clandestine group.'

'But you're no common spy!'

'Ah, Galla, my Galla. I had to see you again.' He pulled me to him, his arm encircling my waist. The warmth of his body almost overwhelmed me and I closed my eyes. His lips touched mine and I opened them to receive his kiss.

'My lady?' came the merchant's wife's voice. She bustled over to the hut. I nearly laughed at Eadmær's expression of alarm as he scuttled round the side.

'Thank you, goodwife, I will be another moment,' I said and fiddled with my belt. As soon as she'd disappeared through the back door of the house, Eadmær grabbed me by the arm.

'Quickly, give me the news.'

'William is determined, almost obsessed. He is building ships day and night. You must prepare strong defences at sea and on the coast.'

'We will fight him with every sinew to the last drop of blood.'

'Very noble, but how many will die?' I challenged him.

'I care not how many of *them* fall. Englishmen will sacrifice themselves if it stops the damned Normans from seizing our island.'

'Gods, Eadmær, why do you men see fighting as the only solution?'

'What? Is this a Roman speaking? Are you only a woman after all?' His fingers ran down my cheek and I shivered at his touch.

'It would be better for all if his ships never set sail,' I retorted.

The next day, we'd made formal farewells of the duke and duchess and sailed from Rotomagus with false smiles on both sides and regret on ours. Downriver a day and a half later, I ordered the sailing master of our ship to stop briefly at the harbour serving Iuliobona. Under the cover of delivering water and fresh food supplies Eadmær and his men slipped on board. Their dozen and our ten Praetorians along with Claudia and myself should manage our planned task if we applied ourselves.

'Why in Pluto's balls' name are we crouching in this blasted hedge in the middle of the night?' Claudia whispered.

'Language, child,' I murmured, but I was concentrating on the Norman harbour below us and trying to count the hundreds of ships bobbing below. The shipyard singing with the noise of hammering and sawing was guarded; torches flared everywhere. Peasants were loading supplies, men-at-arms and horses were crowding and champing on the makeshift quayside. A pity so many people and animals were present.

Claudia and I crawled back about twenty feet from the cliff edge when I heard something move. The creak of a boot. I made a sharp cutting gesture and she froze. Young though she was, like all Romans over sixteen Claudia was trained in basic warrior skills. There it was again, metal rubbing on cloth. The clink of metal on metal. Eadmær and his men were in the valley. If he'd come to join us, he would have whistled the signal. There was no whistle.

I gestured Claudia to crawl directly to the side and edged away on my belly in the opposite direction. Perhaps it was only peasants marauding for food or loot. I eased my *gladius* out and in the shelter of a low shrub came up into a crouch. Then I saw them. A group of three horsemen. One dismounted, knelt and examined the ground.

'Well?' A bad-tempered voice. De Boscville.

'Somebody was here, lord, recently.'

'That damned Roman woman, I'd wager.'

'But they've sailed, haven't they?'

'Supposedly. The duke thinks their threats to hinder our trade were bluster and they can do nothing, but she's a devious bitch.'

'Look, there!' The other horseman pointed in Claudia's direction. The clouds had parted and the damned moon shone through. Pluto swive him. I stood.

'My Lord de Boscville,' I said. 'What brings you out here at this time of night?'

'Seize her!'

I ran, but even the fastest human couldn't beat a warhorse. De Boscville charged and swung at me with his longsword. As I rolled away, he leapt off his horse and, face working in fury, ran at me. He raised his sword aloft, but I ducked under his arm.

Crouching low, I thrust my gladius into his groin, then leapt aside and struck into his side. His sword caught my left arm as it fell, numbing it for an instant. De Boscville was on the ground grunting and struggling to stand. My breath was heaving as hard as my heart hammered. I whirled round to find the tracker on me. I shoved him away, jabbing him in the stomach, then the throat. He clasped his hands to his face with a cry and fell.

The thunder of the third rider's horse was ringing in my head as I turned to face him. I had no breath to run. The horse reared to crush me and I faced death. Then the animal collapsed and the rider fell. Claudia stood there, trembling, blood running down her *gladius* and tears down her face. The horse whinnied piteously. She'd severed its tendons. The rider was unconscious.

I swallowed hard.

'Dispatch the animal.' She stared at me. I nodded. She knelt and drew the blade across the horse's throat. Then she turned round and was violently sick.

De Boscville struggled, but he was mortally wounded.

'Peace, man, prepare to meet your god.'

'You—' he gasped. 'Knew you were poison. Told duke.'

'No, we came to stop you waging a war of aggression, of conquest, against a nation that has done you no harm.'

'William has right. Harold forsworn.' He winced. 'For God and Christ.' His head fell to one side and he passed into the shades.

'I can count several hundred ships, some half complete, others bobbing in the water.' I stopped to draw breath and gulp down ale from the flask Eadmær thrust at me.

'How many hundred?' He frowned at me.

'Four or five at least.'

'Christ good Jesu, we could never match that many ships! And how can we, just over a score of us, hope to destroy even a portion of them?'

'Your men can all shoot straight, can't they?'

'That is a foolish question, Galla.'

'Then be content and wait.'

The Saxons crouched along the edge of the cliff watching the Praetorians ready their portable *manuballistae*, small versions of the classic Roman war catapults. I nodded at the Praetorian commander who instructed his *optio* to distribute boxes of arrows with narrow tubes along the shafts to Eadmær's men.

'What are these?' he ran his fingers along the tubes.

I flinched. 'Do not play with them. They are not always stable, but once loosed, they will achieve our aim.' A cold wave rolled through me, but I had to give the order.

Like a living demon, the loaded arrows and bolts rose in an arc into the dark sky, slowed and then dropped, speeding as they plunged to their targets. Destruction rained down on the harbour that scorched and burnt, that even danced across the water. White flames of death burst out, engulfing the ships, the quay and, Juno save us, the living creatures fleeing from the boats.

'Christ's breath, what is that, Galla?' Eadmær looked aghast at the intensity with which everything below us was consumed. The thunder of explosions and screams reached us across the clear night.

'*Ignis graecus* – Greek fire. A terrible weapon.'

I shut my eyes after ten minutes, weary of watching death and destruction.

'Now we must sail from here as if the Furies themselves were pursuing us. Come.' I took his hand and pulled him away. 'Sometimes we must do dreadful acts to prevent greater disasters, but at least history will record that the Galilean year of 1066 was not the one in which Northman William invaded Saxon England.'

1987

Re-building Roma Nova after Caius Tellus's tyrannical rebellion is pulling on every Roma Novan's personal strength and resources. Young Imperatrix Silvia devotes herself to her country, but she's eighteen, exhausted and lonely.

Andrea Luca is an Italian architect specialising in restoring ancient buildings and is commissioned by the Roma Novan government to supervise the reconstruction. But he arrives early and encounters a young girl on holiday at the famous spa at Aquae Caesaris, west of the city of Roma Nova.

(Set just after the end of RETALIO)

SILVIA'S STORY

It was worse than Aurelia thought. Silvia was completely absorbed in staring out of the window at the broken walls of the Golden Palace. Brooding at the shattered stonework perhaps Silvia realised now, ten weeks after the liberation of Roma Nova and with her family dead, how truly lonely she was.

Formal in a dark green suit, her grey-flecked red-gold hair contained in a chignon, Aurelia Mitela had been in difficult meetings all day. Reconstructing government let alone civil society in an atmosphere of anger, recrimination and guilt was exhausting. She desperately needed a drink and several hours' uninterrupted sleep. But first she was looking forward to the more relaxing weekly catch-up with her young cousin. It would be a relief to talk to somebody both quick-witted and gentle.

'Silvia?' Aurelia said in a soft voice.

The young woman started, blinked and turned away from the window.

'I'm sorry, darling, I didn't mean to make you jump.' Aurelia laid her hand on Silvia's shoulder. 'You've been sitting here by yourself for a while. Did you forget we were meeting?'

'Oh, no!' Silvia shot to her feet. Tears welled up in her brown eyes and she looked stricken with guilt.

'It's all right,' Aurelia said in a soothing voice. 'One missed meeting won't bring the gods on us from Olympus.' Aurelia smiled at her. Silvia was only eighteen, far too young to be the imperatrix of Roma Nova. Poor girl. If her mother hadn't been murdered by the usurper Caius Tellus, Silvia wouldn't have had to take on the responsibility until she was at least in her late thirties. Now she had to lead and heal a divided people after the rebellion and rebuild a ruined country. She looked tired and strained, her red-brown hair flat and dull, and not from the brick dust around them. And her mismatched clothes seemed to hang off her. She was working all hours like the rest of them, but kept her feelings bottled up.

Aurelia beckoned a steward over and asked for refreshments.

'Did you have a proper breakfast? Lunch?'

Silvia looked away.

'I thought not.' Aurelia took the young woman's hand in hers. 'You have to keep up your strength.'

'Don't fuss. You're not my mother.'

'No, I would never attempt to be that, but I'm your senior councillor. If you won't do it for yourself, do it for Roma Nova. You can't afford to faint from hunger or even stumble as you go about. People are so sensitive at present.'

Aurelia sipped her coffee slowly as she watched Silvia peck at a sandwich. She frowned when Silvia only ate half and pushed the plate to the side. Silvia tried to outstare Aurelia, but at the older woman's steady look, she caved in and ate the remainder.

'Good, now we can talk.' Aurelia set her cup down. 'I want you to go to the spa out at Aquae Caesaris for a few days, a week if possible, and—'

'No, I can't. I haven't got time. I must get through these files and see people and visit and inspect things.' Silvia's voice rose with every word.

'Stop.' Aurelia held her hand up. 'First of all, do not interrupt me before I have finished. And secondly, hear me out before you jump in like a barbarian.'

Silvia's face became redder and redder, then she burst into tears. Aurelia handed her a cotton handkerchief and waited. Silvia dabbed her face, sniffed, then looked up.

'Sorry,' she muttered.

'Accepted. You're tired and overwrought. You're trying so hard, darling, but it's been weeks and weeks since you stopped for even a few hours.'

'But there's so much to do.'

'Yes, but you're not much use to anybody when you're too tired to string a few words together, let alone make a rational decision. You can go to the spa tomorrow, do nothing but read a couple of novels, absolutely no state papers. On the third evening, and only if you've had proper sleep the nights before, you can go to the dinner being organised by the reconstructed *curia* there. You might think it would be boring listening to a crowd of local councillors. However, they would love to meet you.'

'Of course,' Silvia said with a huffy tone. 'You know I never shirk my duty.'

'Yes, I know, darling, but you'll not only boost their morale, it will be an excellent opportunity for you to glean information at first hand for us about their immediate concerns.'

The next morning, Silvia set off in the refurbished staff car Aurelia had driven when she'd commanded the forces liberating Roma Nova not three months ago. Fuel was still scarce as the refinery tanks blown up by Caius Tellus's thugs were under repair, but the military had its own supply, currently imported from New Austria.

A small detail of Praetorian guards drove behind Silvia, but most people were only too glad to see the young imperatrix as testified by the waves and hats off as she passed people travelling on the road. A few looked on solemnly or even frowned, unsure whether the restoration *would* bring stability. Overriding the protests of her Praetorians, she made frequent stops to talk to people, even if it was for a few minutes. She knew even at eighteen that every heart and mind had to be reassured after the past two brutal years.

At the spa, the manager greeted her and showed her to her rooms.

'We're a little untidy, *domina*,' he said. 'But the waters are flowing and clean. You can be entirely private as I will arrange for your meals to be sent to your suite.'

'Oh, may I not eat in the dining room?'

The manager exchanged a look with the woman Praetorian behind Silvia who shook her head. 'I'm sure you would be more comfortable in your own quarters, *domina*,' he said. He smiled as a father would to a cherished daughter.

'I've spent the past eighteen months cooped up in exile,' Silvia replied. 'Now I would like to talk to my fellow Roma Novans here in Roma Nova.'

'We only have a few guests at present, including foreigners, although I am expecting further arrivals on Monday.'

'Then it would be wasteful to serve me separately.' She gave the manager a speculative look. 'I would think you are probably still short-handed from the war.' He hesitated. 'Well, that settles it,' she said briskly. 'What time is supper served?'

Praetorian Franca Oppia hunched over on an uncomfortable plastic chair at the side wall of the swimming pool area. There were chips in some of the tiles and an unhealthy brown stain in the corner of the ceiling, but the water was sparkling and clear enough for her young charge to enjoy herself. Franca hoped the new imperatrix wouldn't turn out to be as pig-headed as her mother had been, though. That had led to nearly two years of terror and despair. Franca fidgeted with the button on her radio. Should she call back to HQ for clarification about the security risk of letting Silvia eat with unscreened civilians? Or was she being paranoid? Paulus and Grex were on patrol outside this evening. Oh, to Hades with it! She, Franca, would be in the dining room at a table by the door and could watch everybody as they entered. Why not let the kid relax for a change? That's what she was here for, after all.

At the door, Franca glanced round the dining room. Two elderly ladies were sitting at the communal table in the middle of the dining room. At the window, two couples, Germanic speakers, were talking heartily to each other, completely oblivious of anybody else. Satisfied, she nodded at the manager who came forward to greet Silvia and gestured her to a single table also by the window, but away from the noisy group.

'If you don't mind, I shall sit with these ladies,' Silvia said and slipped into a seat next to one of them at the communal table before the manager or Franca could say anything. She said a polite good evening, whisked the linen napkin off the table and onto her lap.

'And you're very welcome, my dear,' one of the elderly ladies said. 'It's lovely to see a youngster out and about. My sister and I lost our niece in the rebellion.' She looked down for a moment, blinked behind her thick-lensed spectacles, but looked up within a moment or two.

But Silvia hadn't missed the tear rolling down the woman's face. She grasped her hand. 'I'm so sorry to hear that.'

'Well, you don't want to hear us maundering on. We're celebrating. This is our first little holiday since that beast Tellus took over. Good riddance to him and Juno bless our young imperatrix. What did you say your name was, dear?'

Silvia hesitated, then crossed her fingers under the table against the lie and replied brightly, 'Justina.'

Silvia slept in the next day and passed the rest of the morning swimming, then being massaged and pampered. The spa hadn't been able to restock their stables yet – their horses had been confiscated by Caius Tellus's nationalists – so she hiked along the bridle path in the afternoon with Franca in tow.

At dinner that evening, Silvia talked and laughed with her two new friends, slightly shocked at the range of their dirty jokes but nevertheless chuckling at them. She was so absorbed that she didn't notice how well she was eating.

She'd just finished her main course and as she took a sip of wine she glanced over to the door. Franca had relaxed her usual stern expression and was sitting quietly just to the side of the entrance. Silvia found the Praetorian pleasant enough, but was sure she was reporting back daily to Aurelia. She shrugged. It couldn't be much fun for Franca watching her eat, swim and sleep with the only physical diversion walking in the spa grounds.

Silvia turned back and was laughing at a joke made by her new friends when her eye was caught by another guest entering the dining room; a man, early thirties, tall, slim build, brown hair and eyes. A pair of light gold-rimmed spectacles perched on the nose in his thin face. She saw Franca scrutinise him, then raise an eyebrow at the dining room manager who hurried over. But Silvia, wine glass in hand, stopped mid-laugh and stared at the man. He stared back.

The colour crept up Silvia's neck and into her cheeks. Still holding the young man's gaze, she set her glass down, nearly missing the table top. Her heart thudded and she took a quick breath. Her lips formed an 'O', but she said nothing as if her vocal chords had seized up.

The man's hands fell to his sides, but he didn't move forward. A very faint tinge of pink crept into his face, then it paled.

The chatter in the dining room faded into silence, the manager stopped where he stood and everybody watched. Even Franca stayed in her seat.

A crash in the kitchen.

Silvia blinked, looked down, then up again through her eyelashes and gave a quick smile. She reached out for her glass and drank the rest of the contents in one swallow.

'Are you all right, dear?' one of the elderly ladies said. She glanced at the young man, back at Silvia, then gave the young woman a knowing look. 'Not bad,' she whispered. 'I wouldn't let that one slip through your hands, if I were you. He looks equally smitten.' She nodded towards the man who was now talking to the manager, but kept glancing over at Silvia.

'I don't know what you mean,' Silvia said, trying to look stern with a face becoming even redder.

'Oh, I think you do,' the woman said. She stood, walked with precise steps over to the manager and the young man.

'I see you're alone, young man. Come and sit with us at the long table. My sister and I love talking to new people. Two in one evening is an unexpected windfall.' Her eyes twinkled.

'But I couldn't interrupt you,' he said in Latin with a sing-song accent.

'Not a bit of it. The long table in any eating place in Roma Nova is open to all,' she replied and with the privilege of age took his arm and propelled him to the table.

Silvia fidgeted in her seat as he sat opposite her. He shot a glance at her, then looked away as if embarrassed. She studied the stranger's face as he read the menu. Somehow, in some way, she knew he was no stranger. Confused, she said nothing.

'Now, young man, tell us who you are,' the younger of the two older ladies asked.

'Andrea Luca,' he answered. 'I'm here to advise on rebuilding some of the public buildings in Roma Nova. I'm an architect, you see, a specialist in ancient Roman construction.'

'Then you're very welcome. The Senate House took a terrible hit. And the Golden Palace was badly shaken according to the news.' She looked from him to Silvia who was giving her apple pastry her complete attention. 'I'd think you'll have a job for life.'

The next morning, Silvia decided to walk through the grounds. She needed fresh air to clear her head and time to think about that extraordinary moment the evening before. She pulled her light fleece on; it might be spring, but there was still a light chill this early in the day.

Franca walked with her, but the Praetorian said nothing, just scanned the immediate area for possible threats. Aunt Aurelia had said as Roma Nova had been liberated barely three months, and although people had been overwhelmingly relieved to see the imperial forces, it was possible pockets of rebels were still active. Silvia glanced at her escort. The other two Praetorians were patrolling the edge of the grounds. She'd overheard Franca giving them their orders before breakfast: 'Protecting the young imperatrix is paramount; nothing and nobody must be allowed to threaten Silvia Apulia.' Silvia sighed. Franca took it all very seriously.

After a few minutes, they reached the ruins of the old bathhouse built in the sixth century, abandoned several centuries later when a new source of warm springs was discovered on the present site. A movement by a wall. Franca tensed as a figure stepped out.

'Oh, Doctor Luca,' Silvia said in a squeak. She coughed. 'What are you doing here?' *Oh, gods,* she thought, *what a stupid question. He's an architect. He has a drawing pad. He's sketching the ruins, of course.*

'Good morning, *signorina*. Did you sleep well?'

'Er, yes, it's so quiet here.'

'Very similar to my native Tuscany. The air is also as pure and full of light.'

'Oh, that's poetic. Is the light good for your drawing?'

'Morning is always best.'

'We're going for a walk,' she burst out. 'Would you like to come with us?'

Franca was not happy. She trudged behind the couple, watching his every move, but he kept a respectful distance from the imperatrix. She'd radioed his name back to HQ last night and he was exactly who he said he was and completely clean. He'd looked at Franca with a speculative eye, but she hadn't volunteered any information. She'd heard Silvia whisper to the Italian that Franca was her chaperone. Well, after the formal dinner at the *curia*, they'd be safely back in the city and Franca would be able to hand over her responsibility to the palace guard. That would be a relief. Watching Silvia in the throes of a crush was slightly nauseating. At thirty-two, Franca was well past that. Her own partner was an engineer – solid, down to earth, practical – and didn't indulge in this lovey-dovey stuff.

The best thing was that Andrea Luca didn't know who Silvia really was.

Andrea travelled on to the city the following day on a bus that had seen better days. But although slow, it ran to schedule and dropped him near the forum. After booking in at his hotel, a modest one, more like a *pensione* in his native Italy, he sought out some lunch. The food in the nearest *caupona* was plain – not surprising after a civil war – but perfectly adequate. He couldn't follow the buzz of conversation in fast street Latin, so he contented himself with reading the news-sheet and watching the other diners. At least a third of them were dressed in military fatigues or wore armbands marked with the word '*Custodes*'. In his schooldays, *custos* meant guardian. Weren't the police here called *vigiles* after the ancient Roman night watch? Perhaps that had all changed as a result of the war. He'd come overland to Roma Nova a few days before his official start date to find his feet. It looked as if there *was* a lot to learn.

Walking round, he was distracted by the warm May sunshine and wondered if he would see that girl again. He'd almost choked when the morning light at Aquae Caesaris had fallen on her hair and struck the fire in it. He'd wanted to bury his head in the rolls of chestnut and take her into his embrace.

The spa manager wouldn't give him her name; her chaperone had looked more like a bodyguard. Women were supposed to be emancipated and independent in Roma Nova, in every sense. Something had been wrong.

Exhausted by traipsing along hard streets, he opted for an early dinner and bed. In some way, he had thought he'd find her as he walked round. Surely, she'd felt the strong pull, the sense of familiarity, the love singing in his heart. She couldn't remain hidden.

He flicked on the television to catch the local news. He would be here for a few months, possibly longer, so he'd better find out what was going on generally.

There she was. She was shaking hands with people in a hospital. A uniformed soldier hovered nearby along with several white-coated medical staff. A woman was introducing her to individual patients. The girl sat at the bedside and said a few words with each patient. And the caption underneath read *'New medical director Doctor Faenia welcomes Imperatrix Silvia to the Central Valetudinarium today'*.

Reporting to the Ministry of Public Works the next day, Andrea received a pass, the key to a small apartment and letters of introduction to the individual site managers. They'd tidied everything up and put any salvageable stone from the damaged buildings aside as he had requested before his arrival. Clearly, his first job was to assess each building and draw up a specification of work required. Armed with his personal copy of Vitruvius's *De Architectura*, he set out his plan.

As he discussed the work for the Golden Palace with the director of services, he couldn't stop looking at the plans of the old section of the palace. The whole building was reasonably compact, but this original part was the size of a modest country villa of the fifth or sixth centuries. Now it had become the private quarters of the imperatrix. Where she lived, protected and isolated.

'Andrea, for the love of Janus, will you stop working and come for a drink? Man, you never take a day off!'

Andrea glanced up. Blandus, one of the junior architects, was a good enough lad who produced excellent work, but keen to get out of the door at five. And he'd tried to drag Andrea out with him over the past few weeks. Andrea went to put his hand out in a gesture of refusal almost automatically. Going out and mixing socially seemed false and useless. There was only one girl he wanted to meet again and she was so far out of his reach it would never happen.

'Look, it's the annual piss-up given by the president of the Architects' Guild and there hasn't been one for three years because of the rebellion. Should be a good night. Well, once the speeches are done.'

'Oh, who's speaking?'

'The minister and director of services. Plus, you'll never guess, the imperatrix is going to hand out awards. Ever seen her? She's pretty fit.'

Dressed in a dark blue suit, shirt, and tie in his university colours, Andrea waited in the lobby of his apartment block. *Insulae* they called them and although not the scruffy tenements of ancient Rome, each one was a little island. Since he'd moved in after his arrival, he'd seen one or two of his neighbours, said good morning or good evening, and that was that.

He pushed the gold-rimmed spectacles up his nose. This is the worst thing he'd ever agreed to. Suppose she saw him? A tiny spurt of anger flared up. Why hadn't she told him at the spa who she was? Perhaps he would have left immediately. Who was he kidding? He fell for her the moment he walked into the dining room. That precious day together was all he was going to get. His contract would finish next spring and he'd be gone. He'd read of her wedding to an aristocrat or foreign prince and he'd line up the bottles of wine and drink himself senseless.

A car horn tooted. Blandus and two of the architectural staff, all dressed formally, had found that rarity, a taxi. At the basilica, they gave their names in and were handed a glass of champagne. From Brancadorum in the east, Blandus said. Andrea sipped and scanned the crowd. Strange to see a sprinkling of women and men dressed like old Romans but wearing spectacles and watches; almost like a toga party, except these were the real thing. One of those figures in dark blue *stola* and yellow ochre *palla*, the director of services, was aiming herself at him. She cut through the crowd with the precision of a marble saw.

'Doctor Luca, how enchanting to see you. Please come with me.'

Andrea shrugged at Blandus and his friends who made faces at him, but he obeyed. At the front of the hall was a smaller group, flanked by a uniformed Praetorian Guard. Andrea's heart speeded up. Surely not. And then there she was, talking quietly to the minister. Her luxuriant chestnut hair was bound up in an intricate plaited affair with a gold circlet woven in, her face was made up carefully to emphasise her brown eyes and full lips, she wore a floor length cream tunic and a purple *palla*, but it was still the same girl who, wearing jeans and fleece, had walked with him in the spa grounds.

Silvia looked up as the director approached, ready to give her a formal smile. Aunt Aurelia had helped her go through senior attendees' backgrounds so she had something pleasant to say to everybody she was likely to meet. Her feet were starting to hurt, but she had to keep smiling. These presentations must end soon. As long as she didn't fall asleep during the speeches…

Gods.

It was him. Her mouth opened, closed then she swallowed hard. A warmth flowed through her. She put her hand out, instinctively.

'*Salve, domina,*' the director said to Silvia. 'I've brought Doctor Luca with me. He's the genius behind the rebuilding work and has been working almost non-stop since he arrived. Have you met him yet?'

Silvia looked up into Andrea's eyes as he took her hand. 'Yes, I've had that great pleasure.'

After presenting his letter of invitation from senior imperial councillor Countess Aurelia Mitela a day later, Andrea was admitted up the drive to the porticoed entrance door of the Golden Palace. He followed the steward across the marble floor of the magnificent colonnaded atrium. His architect's eye couldn't help noting the temporary telescopic props soaring upwards at several points. At the back, down some steps, he passed into a narrower, much older stone hallway with several doors off.

The stone walls were a metre thick and the massive oak doors hundreds of years old; nobody would be able to hear a thing from outside. A Praetorian in a beige and black uniform stood at the oak door set back in an archway at the far end and opened it into a private drawing room. Inside, Aurelia Mitela was sitting on a purple upholstered sofa. Her bright blue gaze settled on his face and searched it.

'Well, young man, sit down and tell me about yourself.'

She poured coffee for them both, settled in her chair and waited.

'My parents are Italian, from Tuscany,' he began.

'Yes, I heard your mother sing when I was a young woman. At the Berlin Opera. Your father is a local medical doctor. But I want to hear about you.'

He blinked.

'It shouldn't shock you that we carried out some background checks before I invited you here. Silvia is not only my ruler, but she was put into my care by her mother moments before she died. Since the rebellion, I am Silvia's nearest blood relative, so as head of the Twelve Families of Roma Nova, I also have responsibility for her as my cousin.'

'I see,' he said. 'Are you warning me off?'

'Not at all. I am merely pointing out the realities. If you are Silvia's choice, then I shall accept that. She has suffered the trauma of losing her beloved parents and brother, her country and her late childhood. She was emancipated at sixteen, but her introduction into adulthood was brutal. She is lonely and needs companionship and stability as well as love.'

'I am determined to give her all of that, if she will accept me.'

'Very well. Let us see how things progress.' Aurelia set her cup down. 'It will mean living here in Roma Nova. Permanently. People will be curious about you, and the newspapers will have a field day. I suggest you become my guest for the moment at Domus Mitelarum. It may stave off some of the speculation for the moment. I shall make it known that I am considering repairs and an extension to my house.' She paused. 'I am delighted that Silvia is happy. She deserves it. But if you break her heart, I shall destroy you.'

By the end of August, Andrea was spending only half his working time at the architects' studio in the city. With Aurelia's blessing, he'd converted a drawing room at Domus Mitelarum into his office. He was fed up with dodging reporters. Some of them had started hanging around the construction sites, annoying the builders, but they gave the journos short shrift in very earthy terms.

Andrea deliberately kept his personal and professional lives separate, but the first week in September, Blandus at last found an excuse to wangle his way into Andrea's new home; apparently, he needed his boss to sign off some plans urgently.

'And this couldn't wait until I was in the town office tomorrow morning?'

Blandus smiled cheekily in reply. 'Phew, this is a bit different,' he said, looking at the tall windows and faded baroque-style decorations.

'The countess said this was her least favourite room because it was over-ornate,' Andrea conceded. 'But the light is excellent.'

'You've found your feet then, moving in here.'

'Perhaps, but in my spare time, I'm working on her plans and she's a hard driver,' Andrea replied quickly.

'My sister saw you at the first of the new concerts at the theatre the other evening. With the old lady and the imperatrix. You all looked very friendly, she said.'

'You were the one who said I should get away from my work now and again.'

'Yes, but—' Blandus paused and studied Andrea's face. 'So the rumours about you and the girl *are* true.'

'What do you mean?' He tried desperately to stop the heat rising into his face. He pulled his spectacles off and tried to look nonchalant. 'You have an overactive imagination, Blandus. Now go away.'

Blandus laughed and fairly skipped out of the door.

Damn and blast him to hell.

'I'm surprised it's taken this long, to be truthful,' Aurelia said. 'You must have been very discreet over the past few months, Andrea. Well done.' She lifted the telephone handset on her desk and asked if it was convenient for the imperatrix to receive her.

At the palace, Silvia ran to Andrea who caught her in his arms.

'What's happened?' she said. She glanced at Aurelia, then back to Andrea.

'They've found out about us,' he said.

'Who?'

'Apparently, the rumour mills are grinding very small,' Aurelia said. 'Don't worry. It's something to celebrate and just what people need.'

Silvia exchanged a worried look with Andrea. He pressed her hand gently.

'Darlings,' Aurelia took one of each of their free hands. 'You'll be protected from the worst of the fuss and it will die down as people become used to it.'

That evening Andrea didn't go back to Aurelia's, but moved into a suite next to Silvia's in the old wing. After supper they sat in the drawing room, his arm about her shoulder, her head nestling on his collar bone.

'Andrea,' she said.

'Mm?' He kissed her hair and wound a strand round his finger.

'I do love you and want to spend the rest of my days with you, but I will understand if this is all too much.'

'Whatever do you mean?' He released the curled hair as she sat up.

'All the formality, the guards, having no freedom, living here. It will be horrible after your life before.'

'*Mia cara.*' He took both her hands in his. 'My life would be truly horrible without you. It's a little strange, but you will guide me. I expect there will be times when I want to scream, but I'll find a deserted room somewhere.' He gave her a rueful smile, but she burst into tears. He pulled her to him and whispered into her ear. 'Let me show you how I love you.' He drew back, bent down and kissed her lightly on the lips. She gasped. He bent down again, but she raised her face and he kissed her passionately, almost crushing her lips. He released her, stood and held his hand out to her. 'Come,' was all he said. They walked silently, arms round each other's waist, to her bedroom.

Aurelia Mitela sat down to her breakfast next morning, picked up the first from the pile of newspapers and scanned the headlines. She flung it back on the table. Of course, it had to be that bloody tabloid *Sol Populi*. She wished it had never reappeared after the rebellion. She grabbed her cup of coffee from the table and headed for her *tablinum*, her office.

The phone rang before she could reach the handset. The palace secretary.

'Yes, I've seen the papers. We'll have to issue a notice. It can go in tomorrow's *Acta Diurna*. Until then, say "no comment". I'm on my way.'

Aurelia grabbed her briefcase and instructed her driver not to stop unless there was peril of life. Predictably, a crowd of newsies outside pushed against the car outside the gates, but the driver ploughed on slowly but steadily, and they broke free. At the palace, a detail of Praetorians was keeping the curious at bay, but waved Aurelia through.

The palace secretary, normally ice calm and efficient, looked flustered.

'Has something happened?'

'No, *domina*, but there's no reply from the imperatrix's intercom phone and the steward has reported she hasn't appeared at breakfast. The door to her apartment is locked. I'm reluctant to send a Praetorian in, but I'm anxious about her safety.'

'I'll go and look myself,' Aurelia said. She turned towards the corridor leading to the private wing. Then it clicked. She burst out laughing.

'Domina?'

'Gods, how stupid we are! What do you think a young woman of eighteen is doing in her rooms when her lover moves in with her?'

Aurelia sat in an easy chair in the atrium, a replacement breakfast finished an hour ago and a fresh pot of coffee half consumed. She worked on her files and waited. At just past eleven, Silvia and Andrea appeared, she with pink cheeks, he with a little smile on his lips. Aurelia smiled in turn when she saw them trying hard not to keep gazing at each other, but failing. Their fingers were completely entwined by the time they reached Aurelia.

'*Salve*, Aunt Aurelia,' Silvia said and kissed cheeks. Andrea nodded, not comfortable about the required protocol.

Aurelia half smiled to herself and looked at her watch.

'Oh! Have you been waiting for us?'

'Now why do you ask that?'

'You're teasing us, aren't you?' Silvia looked worried.

Aurelia laughed, stood and hugged Silvia, then the same for Andrea.

'Sit down, darlings. I wish you every happiness and many fruitful and long days together. I've come to know you over the past months, Andrea, and I think you will be a wonderful companion for Silvia and support her in every way.'

'Thank you, Aurelia Mitela,' he said gravely. 'I am deeply honoured by your confidence. I wish to marry Silvia as soon as we can arrange it.'

Silvia looked at Aurelia and back at Andrea.

'Why?' she asked.

'Because I love you and want to spend the rest of my life with you.' He frowned. 'Don't you want to be married?'

'Not particularly,' Silvia replied. Her face tightened. She took on the look of her mother at her most pig-headed.

Oh, gods, Aurelia thought. Silvia was streets ahead of her mother in intelligence and awareness, even this young, but it had been her mother's stubbornness that had precipitated rebellion and war.

'Silvia, wait a moment,' Aurelia jumped in. 'Andrea doesn't know our way.' She turned to Andrea. 'Silvia doesn't need to marry you, she merely nominates you as her companion.'

'But that's imm—'

Silvia frowned at him. 'It's not immoral, if that's what you were going to say. I know what you do in the West. We don't usually contract formally here.'

'But your parents were married, weren't they?' he said.

'Only two months before my brother Julian was born. And only because my mother was addicted to English romance novels and wanted a formal ceremony.'

Aurelia had rarely heard Silvia speak with such a hard voice, but she heard the fear behind it.

'Well, think about it and talk to each other alone,' Aurelia said and gave Silvia a stern look. 'In the meantime, we have to deal with the now.' And she showed them the newspapers.

By the beginning of December, the sensationalism had retreated and Silvia and Andrea were treated as an established couple. If he had any doubts about their relationship, he kept them private. But Aurelia noticed a certain restlessness about him when he thought nobody was looking. She suggested Silvia invite Andrea's parents for the Saturnalia season; perhaps he would feel more comfortable with his family around him.

'He wants to go to Tuscany and bring them back,' Silvia said. She twisted her fingers together.

'That's perfectly understandable, darling.'

'But they're not old or disabled or anything. And I sent them first class ticket vouchers for Air Roma Nova.' She grasped Aurelia's hand. 'Suppose he doesn't come back?'

'Why on earth do you think he won't?'

'His head accepts how we do things here, but his heart is uneasy. Perhaps we *should* contract formally.'

'Do you want to?'

'It seems like a lot of fuss and bother. My mother was the only imperatrix for generations to go through a formal ceremony.'

'Agreed, but perhaps it's something that is very important to him. His family is traditional. You might consider whether you love him enough to concede on this.'

On the morning of the first day of Saturnalia, the seventeenth of December, Aurelia met Andrea's parents at the airport. As she kissed cheeks with Andrea in the VIP lounge, she whispered, 'Is everything all right?'

'Oh, yes.' He had an air of determination about him as he organised his parents' luggage and settled them in the palace car. Aurelia was amused by his new confidence as he spoke to the Praetorians around him as if he'd done it all his life.

At the palace, Silvia was waiting in the atrium and greetings were exchanged. The vast hallway was decorated with silk swags and greenery and the smell of roast pork and lemons percolated through from the kitchen.

'They start roasting the pig early in the morning,' she said and smiled. 'By the time we sit down tonight, our mouths will be watering. In the meantime, we've prepared lunch in our private wing. Shall we go in for a pre-lunch drink?'

Settled in the small drawing room with a glass of Brancadorum champagne, the small talk flowed. Andrea was attentive, but Aurelia noticed his eyes were gleaming. What in Hades was he up to? Saturnalia was the season of jokes and horseplay, but she was convinced he was too serious to play tricks, especially with his parents present.

He stood in front of the old stone fireplace now full of flames and stretched his hand out to Silvia. She rose in a graceful movement and stood by him, a puzzled look on her face. He kissed her lightly on her lips.

'Mama and Papa, Countess Aurelia, you know Silvia and I love each other. I am living with her in the Roma Novan custom as her companion. But the love of two people has two sides. I commissioned a search and yesterday, in Rome, I collected a very special piece from a friend in the antique business. It is a token of my love that I bring a Roman ring today across the centuries to my own true love.' He brought a tiny leather pouch out of his pocket and slipped a yellow gold ring with twin diamonds into the palm of his other hand. 'I am assured this is very rare, the diamonds do not sparkle as modern ones do, but my love outshines any diamond.'

He took Silvia's left hand and slipped the ring on her fourth finger. He held her hand firmly in his. 'Now with these ancient diamonds for Saturnalia, we are married.' She kissed the ring, her eyes sparkling as she turned to him.

And then she kissed him.

PART II
MODERN TIMES

2011

Newly minted Praetorian officer Carina Mitela and her buddy Daniel Stern, a seconded officer from an allied force, love challenges. Dangerous ones. It's a game to them. But real life gives them a challenge that is anything but a game.

(Set just after the end of INCEPTIO)

GAMES

Why in Hades did I ever agree to this?

A sharp tug on my arm jolted me as we circled again.

Keep your guard up, Carina.

The hot gravel crunched under the soles of my boots as I kept my feet dancing. At the other end of the two-metre chain that bound our left wrists, Daniel caught me in a fixed stare, trying to unnerve me. I glared back. I feinted forward, letting the chain go slack, then jerked it hard and slashed down with my gladius. A thin ripple of blood bubbled onto his arm and he swore. I laughed and felt a wave of triumph.

The intimacy forged by the chain linking his left wrist to mine was intense. Like a lover's embrace, it bound us physically and mentally. Sometimes I even imagined a ripple of energy running up and down the links.

The small crowd cheered, they shouted as they placed bets and heckled. I filtered most of it out.

Jab. Swipe. Lunge.

Concentrate, Carina. Concentrate on the tip of his sword.

He desperately wanted to defeat me. Although he was physically stronger, I was more agile. Sweat ran down my back and between my breasts with the effort of thrusting and dodging.

I must have been mad to do this again. We'd be in the cells if we were caught. A rush of fear mixed with adrenalin as I leapt over the chain to avoid a vicious stab. Gods, he was getting cross now. The blood thrummed through me as I dodged faster and faster. Suddenly, he tripped me and I was on the ground. I pulled him down with me and levered him over my head as I rolled away.

Then he grabbed my foot and pulled me along the ground. My hand was trapped behind my back. Before I could roll and release it, he fell on me, one knee between my legs and kissed me until I lost my breath. *Cheat!* The vulgar catcalls and sexual innuendo drowned everything out. Game over.

He sat up, releasing me. He leapt up, jerking my top arm up as he did and stood there grinning. In that instant I came close to hating him; I did *not* like being beaten. Still grinning like some schoolkid, he stretched his right hand down to help me up. I grasped it and for one moment was tempted to pull him down and restart the fight. Instead I stood up and brushed some of the gravel dust off my fatigues pants. He looked so confident, so carelessly happy. I turned to him, smiled and flexed my leg ready to bring my knee up to use another cheat's trick, when a warning shout broke.

'Patrol!'

Merda.

The onlookers melted like ice in warm wine. He grasped my hand and the bulk of the chain and we ran for it, swords still in hand.

'The hedge,' I gasped. 'By the back wall. Ditch behind it.'

We raced at full pelt and dived into the ditch. My breath heaved in and out of my lungs. Thank Mars, the hedge was thick, dark leaved and rose to a good metre.

'Did they see us?' I whispered.

'Don't think so.'

He unstrapped the leather cuffs of the chain from our left wrists slowly and carefully so it didn't clink. I glanced at his arm. The cut had stopped bleeding. He looked at me and I mouthed, 'Sorry.' He shrugged.

We crouched there listening for human sounds, but only heard birds and insects calling to each other.

'By the way, you are such a cheat,' I whispered. 'That was a whore's trick you played on me.'

'I know,' he agreed. 'Sorry, Carina, but I had to win for once.'

So revenge had part of his motivation for insisting on this match – the male ego in full flight. I rolled my eyes at him and he grinned.

'But, come on, it's only a game,' he said.

Daniel Stern, as a young officer seconded from an allied force, was the next most junior officer to me in the Praetorian Guard Special Forces. We were buddies, becoming friends, helping each other get through the hard training.

He'd walked up to my desk a week ago and proposed the match. It was an illicit pleasure we both relished; chain-link contests had been banned since ancient times because of the high casualty rate. The last time we'd done it, we'd been caught and spent seven days in the cells. Not only that, but the training centurion in charge of the very junior officers had given us an imperial bollocking. I still smarted even remembering it.

Sure, it was dangerous – physically, mentally and emotionally – but the buzz from it gave you a high for days, even longer if you won.

'You're crazy,' I said and glared at him. I glanced around. Nobody was near and we were speaking English together. But that was no guarantee; loads of Roma Novans were proficient in it, certainly the majority in the PGSF.

'Nobody watching will let on – they'll be making too much money taking bets.'

'No,' I said. 'It's just too risky. All we'll need is for one of the guard patrols to come by and we're toast.'

'Oh, come on, Carina, I'm not that thick. I'll find a time when the patrols would be at a minimum. Or somewhere they don't cover that often.'

Then he gave me a smile, his eyelids half closed over his normally bright brown eyes.

'Well, if you're not up to it,' he said, 'then we'd better forget it. I'll let you get back to writing your exacting strategy paper.'

Gods! How underhand was that! Of course, I bit. Which is why we were now crouched down, hiding together in a dirty ditch. We'd been there about fifteen minutes. After another five, I was sure we'd be safe. Then I heard boots crunching along the gravel path towards us. Despite the speed of our flight, I knew we couldn't have left any obvious tracks. Nobody came out this far to the perimeter except the night patrol, but it wasn't night. Once whoever it was had walked on, we'd set off back to the mess and drop the chain, less the leather cuffs, by the transport shed door.

Then the boots stopped.

We froze, shoulder to shoulder, breathing as lightly as we could and not moving a centimetre. Then I smelled Sobranie tobacco; there was only one person it could be.

Pluto in Tartarus.

We exchanged looks. Daniel shook his head very slightly. After five long minutes, the expected voice rasped, 'I know you two limbs of Hades are in there. Shall we be civilised, or do I call a security detail?'

We stayed still.

'Or would you prefer I call the boss?'

Gods, no!

Daniel tried to hold me back, shaking his head.

'Get real, Daniel,' I hissed at him. 'We'll be crucified if he hears about it.' Well, not literally.

I stood up and struggled out from behind the hedge. Daniel followed a few seconds later. Then we stood side by side facing our accuser. We might have been fit and experienced fighters with deadly weapons in our hands that could dispatch a person within seconds, but Vitus, the *primipilus*, chief centurion and the most powerful non-commissioned officer in the entire Guard, looked us up and down as if we were seventeen-year-old recruits. By the time he'd finished, I felt like one. Technically, we might outrank him, but that would be suicidal; he derived his authority direct from the legate. Besides he was the toughest and most intimidating man I had ever met.

'Aren't you two a lovely pair?' His slate grey hard eyes bored into our faces. 'Endangering all that money spent on your training is not the problem. Nor is setting the troops a bad example – none of them is a career flower-arranger, after all. Your problem is disobeying the cardinal rule – not getting caught.' He spat on the path. 'Now I have to decide what to do with you.'

Which is how we ended up on watch duty at the barracks a week later when everybody else was enjoying the opening day of the most exciting games for three years.

We sat across desks from each other, fiddling with screens, bored out of our minds. I flicked balls of crushed paper at Daniel which he batted back. We were alone in an office equipped for twelve, except for a guy tucked away in a corner whose noise-cancelling headphones made him look like a pilot.

'Who the Hades is that?' Daniel asked, pointing across the room. 'He looks far too serious.'

'Paulinus,' I said, checking the roster sheet. 'He's a new research assistant for intel.'

Daniel snorted. 'A techie! Obviously doesn't have a life.'

'Well, he's more interesting than those two sulking outside, sitting on their asses, smoking, or that grumpy Sorasta doing greasy things in the garage. I wonder what *they* all did to catch this duty.'

'He's probably the only one who's here voluntarily.'

I couldn't think of anything polite to say. I was still furious with Daniel, but also with myself if I was honest, for getting into this mess. It was the condition of the deal with the chief centurion that we had to serve our punishment without letting on to anybody that that was what we were doing. The alternative would have been a full disciplinary. I'd had a hard time convincing friends I wasn't crazy when I said I'd volunteered to work today. As for my family, I'm sure they were already signing me up for psychological testing.

I fetched another coffee and wandered over to look over Paulinus's shoulder. He was flicking through the public feeds. He turned, pulled one of the ear cups away from his head and gave me a nervous smile. I smiled perfunctorily back.

'What are you working on?'

'Nothing special, ma'am, just familiarising myself with the system.'

Gripping.

The wall clock showed another five hours to go. Hades!

'Oh!' He gave an almost girlish squeak.

'What?'

'There. On the Dec Max. That silver car. It's been round three times now. He can't be looking for a space – he's passed several good ones.'

'Have a look from the other end,' I said. 'But go back twenty minutes.' Sure enough, the same car, but also a figure tracking it but trying not to look as if she was. I switched back to the real-time screen. There she was again, wearing a cherry-coloured coat and fidgeting from foot to foot. Was she a working girl? Hardly likely to find any clients in the middle of the deserted city centre today. What else could she be doing? Or could she be a lookout? Or the scarabs?

'Daniel. Look at this.'

He studied the time-lapse sequence on the screen in fast-forward mode then brought up the *custodes* shared site on another monitor. Our esteemed police colleagues, which almost everybody called scarabs after the dung beetle because they also had to sort through piles of shit, were pretty good at posting on the Joint Watch list. If they were running anything, we'd see it.

'No operations by the scarabs. They're all at the games, lucky sods.'

We looked at each other, sensing escape. Daniel went out to drag in the two guards loitering outside. Being on standby detail in full kit today must have been even more boring than sitting watching screens indoors.

'Names?' he said as they stood in front of him. I handed him the roster sheet. 'Ah, Tolia and Pincius.' He pointed to our desks. 'Sit here and watch that woman and the silver car.' He looked over at the techie. 'Paulinus, you're in charge. We'll relay anything through you.' Poor guy, he looked nervous, but he nodded at Daniel.

In the locker room, Daniel and I quickly changed into civvies.

'You sure we're not deserting our posts?' I said. 'Shouldn't we stay here and send *them* out?'

'Absolutely not. Don't you want to get out of here?' He grabbed his jacket and grinned at me. 'All guards are trained in surveillance. Even that sulky pair can handle watching a screen.'

It was scarcely ten minutes on foot, so we tabbed it, slowing at the crossroads with the Dec Max. Then we sauntered onto the street hand in hand, like a couple, laughing and gazing in the windows of the closed shops. I spotted the cherry-coloured coat first. The woman was around thirty, long brown hair, no handbag – that was strange. Daniel fished out a cigarette, did a mime pretending he didn't have a light and approached her. She scrutinised his open, smiling face, decided he was genuine and produced a lighter from her pocket.

We wandered on, turning at the next corner. The shop entrance was cut away, so we could look back and watch unobserved.

'Well?' he said.

'She doesn't look like a user,' I replied. 'She's skinny, almost gaunt, but her skin and eyes are too clear. Exchange of some kind, possibly pickup?'

The silver car came round again, stopped and a window opened three quarters. A hand beckoned her. *Jupiter's balls!* It was the deputy station chief from a Latin American embassy. I clicked away on my camera phone over Daniel's shoulder as she got into the car, which disappeared. Unbelievably, it came round again. Didn't they teach them tradecraft or were they contemptuous, knowing the city was closed down for the holiday?

The woman was dropped off at the far end of the street. She now carried a leather shoulder bag. The car disappeared. She looked around once, but we were well hidden in the shop doorway. We followed her to a kiosk just off the forum; it must have been the only one open in the city centre today. I adjusted the superzoom function on my phone and focused on her hands. She spent half a minute selecting a magazine, then reached in her purse for her money. As she held out a five *solidi* note, I caught her on camera passing a small envelope to the owner.

As she walked away, I nodded, and Daniel radioed Paulinus.

'Control, Lynx One. Keep your eyes on that kiosk. Send me a close-up the second anybody else appears. Oh, and send an unmarked pickup to our position. Out.'

I followed the cherry-coated woman at a distance with Daniel as backup, ten metres behind me. After two further streets, I closed the gap and came right up behind her.

She glanced round. Her eyes widened when she saw me, and she broke into a run. But I was faster. I grabbed her arm in such a firm grip she gasped.

'Stop. I am Lieutenant Mitela of the Praetorian Guard. You are under arrest for suspicion of passing information between a foreign diplomat and a Roma Novan. You must come with me.' Daniel had caught up and took her other arm.

She started to protest, but her voice died away when she saw how determined we were.

'My child. I must go home to my child.' Her voice was piteous.

'What's your address?' I said. 'We'll send somebody round. Or is there a neighbour?'

She shook her head and said nothing. We waited for a few moments, but she wouldn't say anything. We marched her into a side entrance where Daniel cuffed her and read her her rights. The car sent by Paulinus eventually arrived, driven by the grumpy mechanic, Sorasta, still in her coveralls. The woman in the cherry coat's stricken eyes gazed out of the back window at us as the car drove away. Well, we'd get to the bottom of that later once she'd been ID'd and processed.

Daniel gave a brief snort of laughter at the bottle of water I bought at the kiosk. 'What are you going to do with that? There's no caffeine in it.'

'Maybe not, but I got a good look at the kiosk owner. Her stuff isn't anything special. No games stickers or hats or other souvenirs, so I can't see any logical reason why she's open today. There hasn't been a customer in the past half hour beside me.'

We were leaning against a side wall in a passageway but the kiosk was in direct line of sight. We waited. After another twenty minutes, a dark-haired man with strong features approached the kiosk. I zoomed in on his hands with my phone camera as he bought some cigarettes. There. There it was – a brown envelope along with his change. I clicked like crazy. His movement was very slick – he had to be another spook. I checked my shots. Yes, the images would look good when we issued the *persona non grata* order.

I grabbed Daniel's hand and we walked towards him. Daniel muttered into his tooth mic to order another pickup vehicle. As the man turned the street corner, we pounced.

He pulled out a handgun. Before he could raise it I lunged and grabbed it. He aimed a vicious kick at me. I dodged, but it partially caught me. I gasped and threw my entire weight on him, flooring him. He shouted a string of harsh words. While I was recovering my breath, Daniel turned the man onto his front to cuff him but he managed to thump Daniel in the eye. Fury on his face, Daniel shouted almost direct into the man's ear. The gods knew what Daniel said – it sounded like something in Arabic. Our antagonist's shoulders flopped and he stopped struggling. Picking up the kiosk owner was a cinch in comparison.

Back at the barracks, we handed the man and the kiosk owner over to the custody suite team, who were disgruntled at being interrupted watching an exciting match on their screens. We left them to do the preliminaries with shouts of 'I have diplomatic immunity! I insist on being released immediately. I want my phone call' fading away as we went back upstairs. I wrote up the report and Daniel downloaded and logged the photos. Paulinus goggled to have seen his first live operation, but settled down to running ID and background checks on our catch. Well, everybody's a virgin once.

I found a dose of coffee and, back in uniform, we went to the custody suite to chat to our guests. I glanced at the duty sergeant's name badge. 'Okay, Sergeant Gabinus, who do we have first?'

'Any chance of getting this diplomat out of our hair?'

Daniel and I exchanged glances. He shrugged.

'Sure. Wheel him in.'

The personification of outraged bravado came in and sat huffily on the chair opposite me. He'd been searched and ID'd as the third commercial attaché at a Middle Eastern embassy. I sighed inwardly. Didn't they ever try to think up an original cover function?

'You have been detained due to engaging in activities incompatible with your diplomatic status,' I intoned the formulaic words. 'You will therefore be deported within the next twenty-four hours as *persona non grata*. You will be escorted directly to the airport from here. An officer from the Department of Justice will contact your embassy and deliver the order. In the meantime, you will remain as our guest. Do you understand?'

He launched into a volley of shouting, which I couldn't follow as he was speaking his own language, but I knew a threat when I heard one. After a few moments, I switched off. When he stopped to draw breath, Daniel's voice came out of the shadows behind the diplomat.

'We could, of course, put you on a plane to somewhere a great deal less friendly. I'm sure some of my former colleagues would love to talk to you.' Then he added something in the same language he'd used before and the man blenched.

I left Daniel watching the diplomat write his life story. I decided to leave the kiosk owner until the morning but, intrigued about the woman in the cherry coat, I asked for her to be brought in next.

'She's a funny one, ma'am,' Gabinus said.

'Oh?'

'Her clothes are shabby and one of her shoes has a hole in it. There's no sign of her on my system. Not on the *custodes* one or public service. She's a nobody.'

'Weird. Okay, I'll have Paulinus in intel check her out. Back to you soon.'

Paulinus didn't have much either.

'I've run her prints as well as your images, ma'am, on social security and health, but there's a confidentiality marker blocking the information.'

'Damn. She's opted for no system access.' All very well for citizens' rights, but a pain for law enforcement.

'Shall we run them on PopBase?' He looked up at me.

The total population database held everything about everybody. Access was very tightly controlled, and it could only be used under certain restricted circumstances by qualified, named individuals. I certainly wasn't cleared, nor was Daniel; we were operations, not intelligence.

'Sure, that would be wonderful, but we don't have anybody here who can authorise.'

'Well, I can.' He glanced at me sheepishly.

'You, Paulinus? Really?'

'It only came through yesterday as part of my induction. I haven't tried it solo yet.' He scratched his thigh with the tips of his fingers.

'Then now's the time,' I said. 'Go!'

Overcoming his initial nervousness, Paulinus found her within minutes – I was impressed.

'Mariana Sila, twenty-nine, Roma Novan, unemployed, one child, lives on the Via Septorum,' he read out. 'Two debt judgements, no immoveable property. Oh! It looks as if her bank are about to zap her credit access and her landlord—'

'Okay, Paulinus, I get the picture. Give me her full address, then log off.'

He looked surprised, but I felt uncomfortable when this kind of unnecessary information was openly exposed. The poor woman had enough problems without us gloating over her money difficulties.

I ordered one of the standby guards to fetch water and some sandwiches from the staff machine to Interview 4 and asked Gabinus to bring Sila in.

Now she wore the standard yellow custody tunic she'd been given after being searched. She looked dejected; her eyes were empty of any expression. Seeing her close up, I noticed her hair was dull and there was a sallow tone to her skin which stretched over her cheekbones. Gods! The woman looked half starved. When the sandwiches came in, her eyes fixed on them like heat-seeking missiles locking on to their target.

I kept half of them on the tray and pushed the other half towards her with a plastic mug of water.

'Eat slowly, I don't want you being sick.'

She glanced up at me, made no movement, looked again, then her thin hand darted out, grabbed the half-sandwich which she devoured in a few seconds. The water went down as quickly.

'Now, Mariana, what have you been up to?'

No answer, just a furtive look at me, then down at the plate.

'Let's put it this way. We take a serious view of people passing confidential information from one set of foreign spooks to another. If we let them get away with this, they may just get the idea they can do this to us.' All her attention was on the second sandwich; she stared at it as if it was treasure. 'Mariana, listen to me,' I continued. 'You'll probably get five to eight years on these charges, depending on what the judges have had for breakfast.'

She just stared at the plate. Gods, when had she last eaten?

Then I tried a whore's trick of my own. 'Do you want your child to grow up without her mother? To be adopted while you're in prison? She won't remember you after eight years.'

'No!'

'So, tell me, how did it begin?'

She burst into tears and sobbed her heart out.

A while later, Daniel slipped into the room as we were finishing. I gave her the second sandwich, poured her another mug of water and we left her there.

'Paulinus, dig me out the duty social welfare officer covering Septorum.'

'What are you doing?' Daniel asked, perching on the edge of my desk.

'That poor bloody woman down there is starving, trying to survive on nothing and feed her child. That's why she took the money for being the messenger. Why the Hades hasn't it been picked up?'

We lived in a prosperous country where nobody needed to starve; we had good safety-net provision. How had this happened? Paulinus came up trumps and I dialled.

'What concern is it of ours?' Daniel asked.

'If you need to ask, then there's not much hope for you.'

He snorted and walked off to his workstation, but I noticed he listened in to my conversation.

'Duty officer? PGSF Watch here. We've picked up a suspect for a Class 2 offence, but we think there's a deeper case here. I'll forward details, but immediately, there's a lone child that needs company, now.' Pause. 'I haven't a clue.' I gave him all Mariana Sila's details. 'Don't you know her?'

I listened some more, mostly excuses. I took a note of the contact's name and email.

'Send somebody along tomorrow morning here to see Sila. And tell them to ask for me.' Pause. 'M-I-T-E-L-A.' Pause. 'Thanks.'

Daniel turned to me. 'We're not a social organisation, Carina. She's been caught in an indictable offence.'

'But she's fallen through the net, off the radar or whatever cliché you want to use. And she has a child. Would you blight her life, too?'

'Okay, fine, but I still think you're too soft.'

'Yes, but if we get Sila to turn informant, we'll not only be able to give her some income until she gets a proper job but push for a community-based sentence.'

'You're taking a big risk exceeding your remit like that.'

'Yeah, reminds me of the one I took last week, but at least today I'm not playing games.'

2019

Legate Conradus Mitelus, commanding the Praetorian Guard, doesn't get out in the field very often. Neither does his wife, Carina Mitela, a newly promoted Praetorian major.

But a personal quest from Imperatrix Silvia allows them to go on their own Roman holiday which leads them into conflict with a strange leftover from Ancient Rome.

(Set between PERFIDITAS and SUCCESSIO)

CARINA AND CONRAD'S ROMAN HOLIDAY

I took another deep breath. Juno knew why – the room stank of stale urine, the mattress was probably full of bugs and I wasn't sure I'd be alive in the next hour in this Roman hole. My shoulders ached from having my hands tied behind me. But spinning round my head along with the after-effects of the drug was my fear that Conrad was no longer alive.

Roma Nova, three days ago

'I don't suppose you fancy going to Rome and posing as a vapid tourist for a few days?' Conrad asked. He tapped the top of his desk with the gold pen I'd bought him last Saturnalia. The March sunlight beaming through the window was pale, but strong enough to throw spots of gold reflections from the pen around his corner office in the Praetorian barracks.

'Are you kidding me?' I said.

'Is that a yes or no?' Even after nearly twelve years of marriage and working together in the Praetorian Guard Special Forces most of that time, he still didn't get what I meant sometimes when we spoke English together.

'Of course. When do I leave?' I said.

'*We* leave tomorrow morning. First to London, then to Rome itself.'

'You're coming with me?'

'Yes. Any objection?'

I shook my head. The idea of several days away with Conrad without children or the formal structure of headquarters military life sounded like Elysium.

'We'll be working.' He looked stern, then grinned.

'Sure,' I replied. But his eyes were full of mischief. 'What's the mission?'

The following evening, Mr and Mrs Charles Miller of Connecticut, Eastern United States landed at Rome's Transtiberina Airport on a flight from London. Although Conrad was impersonating Chuck Miller to perfection, I was a little worried about using the Patricia Miller legend as it had been so flimsy when we'd first posed as the American couple years ago. Conrad assured me the intelligence admin staff had fleshed it out in the intervening years. Apparently, we were now middling successful antiquities dealers.

He rubbed his finger in a circular motion around the same spot on the window of the Leonardo Express which would deposit us at Rome Termini station. His other forearm rested on the seat separator touching mine. Although the train noise would have covered my normal speaking voice, I bent into him and whispered into his ear.

'Is this statue thing really so important?'

His look was a mixture of disbelief and impatience.

'Of course. Or we wouldn't be here.'

'Yeah, but why did it need you and me?'

Conrad was the head of the PGSF, the legate. He scarcely went into the field any more. I was a newly minted major appointed to head up operations. Surely a centurion-led team could have done this?

'Because of the personal importance to Silvia.'

'It's not of her ancestor or anything like that, is it?'

'Not that I know, but Cloelia Mitela, the war hero who negotiated the treaty with the Eastern Romans, was the great granddaughter of Lucius Apulius. She was named after the original Cloelia who escaped from Lars Porsena in the early Republican era.'

Imperatrix Silvia was not only our efficient ruler and somewhere along the line a cousin of mine, but had been Conrad's patron and lover before he'd met me. They shared three children. I liked Silvia, but I always wondered how much of an emotional bond she and Conrad still had.

'Um, isn't this all bit tenuous?' I said.

'Yes and no. We're technically on leave. Silvia didn't want to make it official but thought we'd be interested in doing it for family reasons.' He glanced at me. 'But we can draw on any resources we require.'

Terrific. We were off on a legendary wild goose chase.

In a tiny side street off the Via dei Coronari, not far from Agrippa's (or Hadrian's) magnificent Pantheon, Conrad stopped and looked up and down the cobbled street of tall golden stone and flaking stucco buildings. No sign of life apart from the occasional metal clad planter with evergreen climbing plants, a bicycle propped up near an arched doorway and iron grills on ground floor windows. A skinny cat emerged from a building, inspected us, then stalked off.

Two steps on, Conrad rang the bell on a narrow door next to a tiny shop window displaying silver artefacts.

'Signor Miller?' An elderly woman with fine hair brushed back into a loose bun opened the door. The hand she held out in greeting was covered in brown age spots, but strangely few wrinkles. 'And Signora Miller, I presume?' She smiled at me, a little condescendingly, I thought.

'Hi, Signora d'Alessi.' Conrad threw out his hand and an all-teeth smile. She shook his hand quickly but firmly.

'Please, come in.' She relocked the door by treading down on a floor bolt and flicking a standard mortice lock by the silver handle. The little shop was discreetly lit by flower-shaped wall lights and cabinet lights in the glass counter and display cabinets. She beckoned us through a door at the back of the shop almost obscured by a large bookcase. Inside was a sitting room out of a nineteenth-century drama movie set but with a modern silver and black computer perched on an old polished wood keyhole desk. On the table was a dark wooden box around twenty centimetres square with a tiny silver key protruding at the top of one side.

'Well, here it is.' She turned the key and the front dropped down to reveal a cloth bag. She untied the drawstring and the silky material fell down around the base of a silver statue of a horse and its rider, a girl in a long tunic and cloak. The horse in mid gallop was straining its neck and the girl was leaning forward, her hair streaming behind her. In the pale yellow light reflecting the crimsons and deep greens of the room, she looked almost alive.

'Oh, wow,' Conrad said in character. But his eyes gleamed in genuine appreciation. 'My client is going to be very excited.' He opened his laptop bag which had served as his flight bag and brought out a pair of white cotton gloves and jeweller's loupe which he stuck in his eye.

'May I?' he asked Signora d'Alessi.

She waved her assent and glanced at me. I gave her my best bland smile. As Conrad bent over the silver statue doing his dealer act, I looked around the room. Oil paintings and furniture crowded the walls and floor. Maybe she had downsized from something grander. Her file said she'd married her cousin, another d'Alessi; they'd belonged to a family prominent here in Rome a hundred years ago before the Great War of the twentieth century. She had no children and was the last of her line. The window at the side, framed in red velvet trimmed with gold, gave onto a passageway which let some natural light in, but no view except of a crumbling stucco wall.

As Conrad unbent from examining the statue, I was still wondering why we'd been dragged into a simple errand like this. Of course, being away with the man you loved in a romantic place like Rome in the spring was pretty attractive.

'We agreed a price, didn't we?' he said to Signora d'Alessi. 'Subject to seeing it. And it's as promised. I'll have funds, including shipping, transferred immediately from New York into an account of your choosing.'

She hesitated. 'There is another party who has expressed interest.'

Conrad gave her a long look, the kind he aimed at juniors trying to wriggle out of taking responsibility for their misdemeanours.

Pink tinges appeared under her cheekbones, but she gave him it back in a cold voice.

'I would not dream of breaking our agreement, Signor Miller. That is not my way. But I should warn you that the other people were extremely persistent.'

'I was under the impression this was handled with maximum discretion. How did they know it was for sale?'

'I don't know,' she said. 'My cousin approached me on behalf of her father, Roberto Neri. He lives in the family estate up in the Sabine Hills and only thinks of his vineyards. Apparently, he wants to buy a new processing plant. The piece has been in their family for hundreds of years. Legend has it that their family goes back to late Roman times.' She gave a delicate shrug. 'Unlikely, but they seem to like the nostalgic idea.'

'I guess there must still be some Romans left around Italy,' I chipped in and laughed.

'No doubt, young woman,' she retorted. 'But the only genuine ones we know of anywhere are in Roma Nova and they are a strange people.'

'Oh?'

She turned towards Conrad without answering me. I was about to pursue it, but a movement in the window caught my eye. I strode over, but saw nobody, just a blonde woman turning into the Via dei Coronari. The sunlight was so strong there, I couldn't make out her features, just long curling hair.

'I will place the statue back in my safe room,' Signora d'Alessi said with that tone people used to finish a conversation. 'Please arrange to collect it tomorrow or the next day. I want such a precious thing off my premises as soon as possible.'

'Well, she was a bundle of fun,' I grumbled as we walked back to our hotel.

'Just an embarrassed ex-aristocrat dealing with the brash New Worlders. Let's get a drink. I'll just text Silvia.' As we walked on, he bent his head, tapping away on the glass surface of his smartphone. I couldn't see as the sunshine was too bright, so I looked at the classy stuff in the windows of the shops we passed. Then I saw her.

'Uh, Conrad,' I murmured. 'I don't want to spoil things, but I think somebody is tailing us. Woman, early thirties, sunglasses, bandeau in dark brown hair, light blue jeans, cream shirt. If she isn't following us, then she's acting very strangely.'

'*Merda*. Well, let's get that drink, then go for a wander.'

As we drank our *spremuta di limone* in a square nearby, our tail seemed to have vanished. Maybe I'd been imagining things, but I didn't think so. I'd been an intelligence officer for long enough. We paid and set off to the Pantheon, still a wonder of Roman architecture. Once through the darkness of the entrance portico, we entered the enormous circular space. At the top, the *oculus* opened the way to the gods. Then I glimpsed her again. No bandeau in her hair which she'd now piled up on top of her head. Large hoop earrings swung as she moved her head, the shirt, tight at the neck, was now mostly covered by a pale denim jacket. But her walk gave her away.

'Five o'clock,' I mumbled as I stretched up my arm as if pointing to something.

'Okay, let's circle her and see what she does.'

We split up. I walked round the edge, marvelling at each marble panel, Conrad walked straight to the altar ostensibly to look at the silver icon Eastern emperor Phocas had given to the Christians when he turned the Pantheon over to them in the seventh century. Apparently, Roma Nova had objected strongly, sending Phocas an emissary to plead against it, but had failed. Well, they'd looked after the building over the centuries, but still…

Switching my phone to front camera, I pretended to take photos of the fabulous domed roof, but I was watching the woman watching Conrad. He took a tourist picture, then made his way out of the Pantheon, under the portico and back into the sunshine. She followed. As I followed her, back to the Piazza Navona, the site of Domitian's first-century stadium.

Conrad paused by the famous fountain in the centre and dutifully took a photo. The woman mingled within a party of tourists, but kept her eyes on Conrad. He cut southwestwards to the Campo de' Fiori and still she followed. He wove between the market stalls selling every kind of flower, olive, honey, t-shirt and vegetable you could imagine. I almost lost him visually but tracked him on my phone. Where in Hades was he going? A ping alerted me that we should end it here. He left by the south-east corner with his tail a few metres behind. I closed up on the woman and as he dodged in a side street, I was right behind her. I grabbed her arm and pushed her against the wall. Conrad crossed his arms and frowned at her.

'Okay, you,' I said in my best American. 'Why are you following my husband?'

Her eyes shifted from me to him, then back again.

'I not know what you mean.' Italian from her accent.

'Sure you don't,' I drawled. 'Now tell me the truth. Are you stalking him? Or are you planning to rob him?'

She shook her head. I shook her by the shoulders. But she said nothing.

'Okay, we'll just go to the police and file a complaint.'

Conrad grabbed one of her arms and I took the other.

'Okay, honey,' he drawled. 'Which way?'

I checked my maps app.

'About two hundred or so metres away – Piazza della Trinità dei Pellegrini. Oh, and they speak English.'

She struggled all the way, but Conrad had a firm lock on her and frogmarched her through the stone doorway. We gave our details and I was relieved that our EUS passports stood up to scrutiny. The *carabiniere* on duty apologised to us again as the woman was led away into the back of the station. His older colleague stood to one side silent and watchful until we were ready to go.

'One moment, Mr Miller. A question.'

'Yes?'

'You and your wife seem very capable, more than the average tourist. I'm curious about that.'

Crap.

'No mystery, sergeant,' Conrad replied smoothly. 'I did service with our national guard for a few years and my wife was a team leader in the New York Kew Park Corps. She was great at tracking missing kids or people up to no good.' He grinned at me.

'I see.' He gave us both a measured look.

'So what happens now?' I asked, partly to divert him from going anywhere else with his questions. 'Do we need to go to court? We're only here for a few days.'

'No, Mrs Miller. We will check the woman's background then decide what to do with her. Your statements will be enough.'

'That's great, sergeant,' Conrad added and put his arm round my shoulders. He pressed his fingers into the top of my arms. 'I think we deserve a good lunch now to get over this.'

The older cop nodded and watched us until we left the office counter.

As the sunshine outside hit us, I whispered, 'You are one devious so-and-so.'

'Always stick as close to the truth – basic intelligence training.' He laughed.

'Yeah, but I'm sure he didn't believe you. If he checks up he won't find me or you on the EUS records.'

'Perhaps, but we'll be back in Roma Nova before he gets any reply from the EUS.'

'What if he puts us on their internal records system and one of your GIS buddies recognises your photograph?' I'd never trained with the Italian special forces, the *Gruppo di Intervento Speciale*, but Conrad had, and just last year.

'Unlikely,' he replied. 'Anyway, Michele would keep his mouth shut and contact me before doing anything official.'

'But we still don't know why that woman was following you. There are far easier marks for pickpockets and we were carrying secured bags. I just have the feeling it was something to do with that damned statue.'

'Really?'

'What else could it be?'

'Okay, I'll see if I can get a guard from the legation to watch d'Alessi's shop if you're that worried.'

Next morning just after eleven, we were on our way back to the little shop to pick up the statue. We didn't need an export permit as it wasn't on any heritage list. Our rental SUV was parked nearby in a tiny square and we'd booked seats on that afternoon's flight to Vienna in New Austria. We were being ultra cautious as we didn't want any direct link to Roma Nova until we had the statue safely out of Italy. In Vienna, Silvia had a private jet standing by at the Wien-Maria-Theresia Airport for the last leg home.

As we turned into the little street to d'Alessi's, there was no sign of the PGSF guard assigned to watch the shop. Instead a blue flashing light bounced between the tall blocks and blue-clad figures and paramedics filled the narrow cobbled street.

'Mars' balls!' Conrad hissed and grabbed my arm. 'Keep going, but careful.'

'Yes, I do know,' I said, irritated.

It was the same sergeant. Hades. His look could have pierced Kevlar.

'Mr and Mrs Miller. How interesting.'

'Oh, hi. What's happening here?' Conrad said. 'We're on our way to pick up a sale from Mrs d'Alessi. Is there a problem?'

'At least they've given us coffee this time,' I whispered to Conrad. The office walls at the *Questura* were dull and the furniture utilitarian with the Italian president glowering down at us from his official portrait. I tried to ignore the *carabiniere* watching us from beside the door.

'Yes, but I don't like how long it's taking,' he whispered back. 'That clever sergeant will work out that our guard wasn't there by accident or coincidence and the whole thing will blow up in our faces. *Merda.*'

'You showed him the bill of sale, the transfer ticket for the money and our boarding passes. What else does he want?'

'Mercury knows and he's not answering his phone.'

I pressed his hand in sympathy. After another quarter of an hour, the door opened and the sergeant ambled in, a beige folder in his hand. I saw now he was only in his mid forties, but stouter than you would expect for a serving officer. His walk was slow, deliberate even, but his brown eyes darted between us.

'Let me introduce myself properly. Stefano Rossi. It seems only polite as we may be spending some time together.'

'We have a plane to catch today, Sergeant Rossi,' Conrad replied. 'So I hope it won't be that long. But first, can you tell us what has happened to Mrs d'Alessi? Is she okay?'

'Signora d'Alessi is safe and being cared for in hospital.'

'Thank God. Is she badly injured?'

'I cannot give out any details.'

'Well, pass along our best when you see her.'

'What exactly is your connection with her?'

'We were handling the collection of an item for one of our clients.'

'Who is?'

'Sorry, that's confidential.' Conrad gave him the blandest of smiles. 'I guess we won't be doing that now. Pity.'

'What exactly was the item?'

'A silver statue of a girl on a horse. It was in a silk bag in a wooden box. I examined it yesterday in the room behind the public counter to check it out and then confirmed the sale.' Conrad glanced at me, then back to Rossi.

Rossi opened his file and consulted a printed list for a few moments. 'We found the safe door open,' he said. 'Many items were left undisturbed, but there is no sign of your box or the statue.' He closed his file and looked steadily at Conrad. 'A suspicious investigator could think that given the amount on the bill of sale an unscrupulous person with some military experience had the skills to have helped himself and then cancelled the money transfer.'

Conrad's face tightened and he glared at Rossi.

'Now wait just a minute,' I jumped in. 'Are you accusing us of stealing the statue?'

'I have accused nobody, but I'm looking at all possibilities. There is also another strange thing that Mr Miller might comment on. A member of a diplomatic protection detail, fully accredited, was found unconscious in the next street. No injuries, just sleeping off alcohol or perhaps a drug.'

'What's that got to do with us?' I said, trying to look puzzled, but cursing the legation guard in my head.

'A coincidence perhaps?' Rossi said and looked steadily at Conrad. 'I think Mr Miller will need to stay with us for a while.'

'I want my lawyer,' Conrad said in a controlled, but tense voice. 'Now.'

'Hi, Frederick. It's Pat Miller. Something dreadful has happened. You know we're in Rome to close a sale? Well, somebody's stolen the item and the Italian police think Chuck did it.'

I prayed to Mercury that Centurion Marcus Flavius would catch on. I was calling his direct line in the PGSF back in Roma Nova, but standing in a corridor in a police station in Rome when anybody could listen in. At least our call would be digitally scrambled.

'Calm down, Pat, start at the beginning,' Flavius's voice came with a reassuring tone.

'Chuck needs a lawyer now, a top one. Do you have any suggestions? I just don't know what to do!' I could imagine Flavius rolling his eyes at that.

'Okay. Now don't worry. Give me the address and I'll check our contacts and send somebody over.'

'Oh, Frederick, that's such a relief.' I was aware of one of the police watching me. 'Will you call the consulate for me? I'm too upset.'

'No problem, Pat. Now go and sit down and try to stay calm. I'll sort everything out.'

Two hours later, we were back on the street. An extremely confident Italian lawyer with curling salt and pepper hair and a fine line in sarcasm had lambasted the desk officer and wrapped Sergeant Rossi up in so many legal arguments and quoted so many references of the civil code that Rossi must have given in just to get some peace. I'd given Conrad a tearful hug as Pat Miller and he'd patted my back as if calming me. Outside, the lawyer had bowed over my hand and given me his card. He shook Conrad's hand, checked his watch and hurried off.

Arm in arm, we made our way straight back to our SUV but both of us scanned round as carefully as we could for anybody watching us. Only a moped rider buzzing past and an older woman with a woven basket walking sedately along one side of the square gave it any sign of human life. I dropped down as if to tie my sneaker and checked underneath the vehicle. Nothing obvious. Conrad wrenched open the trunk lid to make sure our bags were still there. He slammed the lid down and flung the driver's door open.

'Don't take your temper out driving,' I said. He glared at me, then relaxed.

'Sorry, love, but what a fucking pig's breakfast.'

'Obviously, the "other party" d'Alessi mentioned hasn't taken it lightly. Or perhaps they have. Literally.'

We drove to the airport, checked in the rental, then took another out for a week. We swapped our flight tickets over at fifty per cent admin fee for an open flight.

'Silvia will pay,' he said as we drove back into the city.

Pensione Clara was a total change from the bland international hotel we'd stayed at before. But it had Wi-Fi and I retrieved a message from Flavius with an access code for the central Rome CCTV. Few people realised just how boring it was looking through footage. What else would you do on a mild evening in Rome in the company of your life's love?

An hour and a half later, I jabbed at the screen.

'There!' A woman with curling blonde hair down her back turning from d'Alessi's street into the main one where the CCTV picked her up. Conrad zoomed in and took a screenshot which include the date stamp.

'Flavius will be able to pinpoint her and run an ID check. Let's find our following friend.'

The brown-haired woman who'd followed Conrad was easy to track, even the moment when she changed her hairstyle and put on her denim jacket. Whoever these people were, they were blissfully unaware of public surveillance. Or perhaps they didn't know who we really were. Their mistake.

After a quick meal at the bistro next door, we strolled round to the Piazza Navone just to see if we had silent company, but couldn't see anybody watching us. At the fountain, Conrad pulled me to him and lightly kissed my lips.

'While we're waiting for Flavius, I have a suggestion for passing the next hour or two.' He bent over and tantalisingly slowly kissed me again, this time very thoroughly.

I woke first. Suddenly. Conrad's arms still held me. I lay with my head nesting in that depression at the base of his throat. His skin covered by fine golden hairs was warm with that subtle masculine post-sex scent that made me want to envelop him with my own arms and love him again.

But something wasn't right. I smelled something else. Ether, no, antiseptic. Something hard jabbed me in the head. Gun barrel.

'*Silenzio.*' A woman's voice. I tensed, ready to leap up. One move to grab the gun, the next to disable her. A figure by Conrad, pointing a pistol at his head. 'One move, he dead.' I froze. His eyes jerked open. He thrust out his arm. A muffled shot.

A stab in my arm. Pain. Head swimming. Gone.

So here I was in this stinking room, wearing only a long sleeveless tunic in the middle of March and trussed up like a Thanksgiving turkey. But not with the expected plastic cable ties; it felt like old-fashioned rope. And I was alone. Where was Conrad? Somebody had fired using a silencer. Had they shot him? Was he wounded, or worse?

I wriggled my bare toes and found my ankles tied but hobbled as if to let me walk. A faint outline on one wall indicated a window. I pulled myself up and crossed to the window, trying to ignore the goat shit pellets under my bare feet. Most of the glass in the multi-paned frame was missing; the remaining panes were brown and misty with dirt and neglect. I heard only birdsong and an animal noise. Goats or sheep. So we were in the countryside.

Opposite the window I found a door; rough wood with a heavy iron handle. Of course, it was locked. I pressed my ear against the surface. Total silence apart from my breathing. I shuffled back to the window and turned my back to it. Mentally crossing my fingers, I jabbed my elbow hard against the one pane of glass I could reach. Instantly, I pressed my body against the window to stop the shards falling and making a crashing sound. Very slowly, I pulled away allowing pieces to drop a few at a time. Miraculously, two jagged pieces were still wedged in one of the frames.

Thank Mercury!

Bending over, I thrust my hands back, praying the shard would hold firm in the frame as I pulled my bound wrists back and forth across the its edge. After a few minutes, a sharp cut at the base of my thumb. Something warm trickled across my skin. My blood.

Hades. But I must be near. I stepped away from the window and braced my aching shoulders. One last effort. I took a deep breath, then jerked my wrists apart as hard as I could. Sudden pain, then the last strands of the rope broke. I couldn't help a sob escaping as full feeling returned to my arms and shoulders. Gods, my wrists were throbbing.

But I had to move. Quickly, I tore a strip off my tunic and wrapped it round the centre of the slimmest shard that had fallen from the window. Not much of a weapon, but this was no time to be picky. At least I could cut my ankle bindings.

I had two options; wait for the opposition to come to fetch me or try to escape now. I checked the window. At the edges, the frames were distorted and jammed closed in the middle, but the internal crosspieces looked less robust. I pushed at one and it buckled. Rotten. I reached through. The catch on the shutters groaned as I eased it up. I paused. There was only one lubricant available. Ignoring the smell, I reached down for some goat pellets.

The dawn was just breaking, so it had to be about six, six thirty. Country people started their chores about now, so I needed to move. It would be slow on this concrete and gravel. Once outside, I closed the shutters and saw my temporary prison was one of several outhouses.

Hugging the wall, I crept along to a bigger shed, which contained horses who ignored me. But the treasure there was a row of rain boots. I pulled a pair on with joy. Now to look for Conrad. Please the gods he was still alive.

A farmhouse sat on a slight rise across the yard, but I made for the small copse at the side that would cover most of my approach. The orchard and vegetable garden were bare but gave just enough cover to get to the house. Listening by the side of a window, I heard voices arguing and shouting. Then I registered a male voice. Conrad.

Thank Juno.

'My lawyer will have the police tear this shithole apart.'

'Who says you leave here?'

'You little girls can't hold me.' Gods, he sounded tired. But he was still in character. *Macte!* Then came a slap and Conrad grunted. 'You bitches,' he shouted.

What in Hades were they doing to him?

'*Basta*, Delfina.' A woman's voice. Then some more Italian which I didn't understand. Another grunt from Conrad and the sound of steps. Another woman's voice shouted something with two words I *did* understand – *sua moglie*. It was near enough to Latin *sua mulier* – his woman. They were coming for me.

I scuttled round the side of the house just in time to not be seen by two tall women striding out of the front door.

Okay, Carina, you have about thirty seconds.

I burst into the farmhouse brandishing my makeshift knife and thrust it in the face of the woman bending over Conrad. She jerked up only to find the business end of a glass shard digging into her jugular.

'Don't try anything,' I shouted in English. I pointed to her, then the floor. 'Down. Now.' She hesitated, so I kicked her knee. She collapsed and I place my booted foot on the middle of her back and shifted half my weight onto it. After pulling her jacket down and tying the sleeves together, I sliced through the bindings on Conrad's wrists and ankles.

'Can you stand?' I asked.

He nodded.

'You won't believe who this lot are,' he said and coughed hard. Some blood escaped from his mouth. His face was bruised and cut, but he was standing steadily.

'At this moment, I don't care. We have to go now.'

I could ride competently, but I wasn't an enthusiast like Conrad. And I disliked riding bareback. The gods knew what we looked like; me in a torn and dirty white tunic and rubber boots, he in a dirty stable coat and nothing else. We'd pushed the two women who were on their way to fetch me into the stinking goat pen, then grabbed the horses. Shots whirled over our heads but, thank Juno, none hit us. We raced through small fields and woods, until we burst onto a metalled road. I caught my breath at the beauty before me. We were on the upper edge of a crater and below was a vivid blue almost circular lake. It looked so clear I wanted to leap into it from where we sat on the panting horses.

'Pluto, it's Lake Nemi,' Conrad exclaimed.

'What's that?'

'A site holy to Diana. But more interesting at the moment is that town. It must have a public phone. Come on, stop being a tourist.' He flicked the reins and we rode on.

After making a reversed charges call to Rome, we harboured in woods on the north edge of the town. I kept watch with the horses while Conrad closed his eyes. Large dark shadows surrounded his eyes; he looked exhausted. Had they questioned him all night?

Thirty minutes later, I heard the distinctive noise of powerful engines. As they parked behind the trees as instructed, I peeked over the brick wall and breathed out hard as six people peeled out of each vehicle.

'Senior Centurion Sergilia, Rome legation guard reporting. Sir, ma'am.' She drew herself up and despite the dark chinos and casual shirt, she saluted.

'Stand easy,' Conrad said. 'Thank you for responding so promptly.'

One of the younger troops screwed his nose up. Gods. I must stink from the goat shit. Sergilia jerked her head at him and he scurried off to fetch bottles of water for us. Another brought clothes and sneakers for us. I would just be relieved to shuck off the rubber books that were making my feet sweat. Turning my back, I stripped off the filthy tunic, and used it to rub my hands as hard as I could to remove the greasy crap. Despite the cool weather, I poured a full bottle over my head, followed by another. Conrad had done the same. One of the guards wrapped gauze and tape round my wrists, but they hurt like

Tartarus. As Conrad pulled on fresh pants and shirt, he snapped out his orders.

'Designate two people to stay with the horses. The rest of us are going after a nest of vipers.'

We made one false turning. After another fifteen minutes, we were parking up on the rough approach road to the farm. Sergilia deployed her troops in a pincer movement, two groups of three, plus two to check out the outhouses while she and the young guard waited with us. The house looked quiet, although smoke drifted up from the chimney.

'They had small arms only that I saw and heard,' I whispered as we crept up to the side wall. 'But they're hard in their attitude.'

'No problem there, ma'am.' She grinned at me, then her face became serious as she signalled her troops forward. The first group pushed through the front door. I heard noise from the back. No responding fire. A guard came out of the front door and shouted 'Clear and safe'. All the same, we advanced cautiously.

In the main room, low beamed, but open to the shallow roof, nothing moved. We stood still and listened. Footsteps clattered from the half-floor above. I tensed, but it was only one of Sergilia's people. A fire was nearly out in an open grate, but I spotted some curled papers. Grabbing the tongs from the side, I picked the singed rolls out. Half of it disintegrated, but I took a heap of photos with the phone Sergilia handed me.

'Do you have the facilities to get these papers processed?' I asked her.

'We can do preliminaries, but they'll have to be sent home for detailed analysis. The locals are good, but you can't guarantee complete confidentiality.'

'That's harsh, Sergilia.'

She shrugged. 'Realistic, ma'am.'

'Fair enough. But when people fleeing a scene burn stuff, they're always trying to hide something important. Let's get it underway. In the meantime, we need to do a full search.'

Although I itched to join in, I left it to the troops. They wouldn't want a nosy officer interfering with their search pattern. But Conrad and I examined the finds in detail on the long table in the centre of the room.

The first surprise was that the half-burnt papers were in Latin; archaic Latin, *prisca latinitas*, before the classic rules came in. I handed the phone to Conrad to translate from the photos I'd taken.

'Pluto, this confirms what those bitches were saying.'

'Is this going to be Twenty Questions or do I have to make stabs in the dark?'

'Sorry, love.' He smiled at me and took another gulp from his water bottle. He wiped his lips with the back of his fingers. 'They went on and on about the statue saying it was their property by right and no barbarian should touch it. I couldn't see it, or the box, but I got the impression they had it and were trying to tie up a loose end – you and me. They kept asking who my client was. This was all in English, but I could follow some of their chatter in Italian. Sometimes they even used the odd Latin word.' He looked at me as if searching for reassurance before speaking. 'Don't think I'm mad, but they claim to be spiritual descendants of the vestals.'

'What?' I screeched. Everybody stopped working and looked at me. 'You have to be kidding. The vestal virgins were prim and proper but good women, not violent lunatics kidnapping and beating up on people.'

Conrad flicked his fingers at Sergilia to get the troops back to searching.

'But they were all disbanded by that Greek idiot Theodosius in the 390s. Didn't one come to Roma Nova with Apulius and become the first pontifex maxima?'

'Yes, but they never re-established the College of Vestals there. Women just became priests like the men. *These* women think they are preserving the original.'

'Excuse me, sir,' Sergilia said and waved her hand over the items on the table. 'Is this why we are only finding wood and metal and so on? There's some rubber, like the boots the major wore on her escape, and leather, but we haven't found anything plastic, nor any synthetic fabrics.'

I looked up to the ceiling. The lighting was by candle power.

'Okay, there has to be some kind of altar somewhere with a flame.

And when they left, they would have taken the flame with them in a container or can.'

'Is that phone completely secure, Senior Centurion?' Conrad asked. She nodded and held it out to him.

'I've found this Collegio di Vesta, sir,' Flavius's disembodied voice said. 'It's a charitable and educational foundation, registered in Rome. The two screengrabs from the Rome CCTV you sent me ID the women as Professoressa Delfina Balba and the other as Dottoressa Paola d'Antonio, both Sapienza University of Rome graduates. I'll send you the names of the other board members, seven altogether. They're all well qualified – one's a doctor, another's a graduate chemist.'

'Juno, seven, just like the originals,' I said. 'When was this college thing set up, Flav?'

'The earliest I can find is a mention in the 1790s as a private orphanage and school for young women. I'll message you the registered address. It's not at the farm, but just off the Roman Forum in the city.' The screen was tiny, but I could see his frown. 'One newspaper report from the 1850s is pretty scathing – calls them a load of nostalgic romantics and hints at secret ceremonies and kidnapping children.'

'Juno. What a terrific bunch.'

'They were certainly driven,' Conrad said and rubbed his bruised cheek. 'First we find these women. Then we take back our property.'

'But what do we do with them?'

He shrugged.

'They've broken the law. The obvious step is to hand them over to Sergeant Rossi.'

'But suppose they really *are* the inheritors of Vesta?' I said.

'They are so far off that path I don't think we need to worry.'

After a proper shower at the *pensione* and a solid meal of pasta and salad I felt a hundred per cent better. I persuaded Conrad to take a nap; his face was even more drawn than after his interrogation during the night by the women. I sat at the tiny table in our room, staring out onto the cobbled street and doodled on the pad of notepaper provided for guests. I'd sent a quick report back to Flavius, but was trying to work out our next moves.

Our things at Pensione Clara had been searched, but nothing removed, not even our phones or wallets. It was us they wanted, not our possessions. Did they know we were Roma Novans? Or just think we were the average barbarians? Sergilia's people posing as water company technicians had gone into the Collegio di Vesta's Rome office – three small rooms with empty cupboards – but they'd found nobody there. They had to have a fallback. But where?

'Why are you frowning?' Conrad's voice from the bed, soft with drowsiness, broke into my thoughts.

'Trying to think through the minds of these people. They left the farm, nobody's in their Rome office. Flavius can't find any trace of a vehicle registered to any of them and they're all on the social security system as independent workers or retirees, so no employer records. Where the hell are they?'

He half sat up, propping himself on his elbows, and shook his head.

'I wonder if the pontifex maxima's office at home could help?' he said.

'But they're nothing to do with the vestals.'

'I know, but at this point we need to look down any alleyway, even the blind ones.'

'I cannot believe this!' I shouted out. 'It's too easy.'

'What?' he said emerging from the shower. Droplets of water coating his body reflected the afternoon sunlight pouring into the room. I swallowed hard as I watched him advance. If only we didn't have this damn statue thing to pursue…

'What?' he repeated.

'Oh. Sorry. Gold from the P. Max's office. The original vestals had outreach sites. One at Bovillae on the Via Appia. It's now called Frattocchie, part of a town called Marino. We must have driven straight through it this morning. According to the P. Max's people, religious rituals were transferred there from Alba Longa in 658 BC including the cult of Vesta – *virgines vestales Albanae*. They may be hiding out there, but there's nothing to see, just a Christian monastery building on what the Internet map calls 'a religious site from antiquity'.

'Hm. Any other options?' Now he had some clothes on I could concentrate.

'Yep.' I tapped to the second saved screen. 'How about going right back into history?'

'Try me.' He bent over me and wrapped his arms round my shoulders. The warmth of his skin was exhilarating, but I managed to focus back on my screen.

'Lavinium. It was pretty big in its time, but super significant for being where Aeneas the Trojan landed. And the vestals had a small site out there since they were founded. And rising behind the archaeological museum which has original ruins of parts of Lavinium from several centuries BC, there's a flat-topped hill with a farmhouse on it. And in one of the fields the satellite image shows what looks like a stone enclosure, like the religious one at Virunum. And...' I twisted round and grinned at him.

'Go on, you tease.'

'Flav confirms the land registry details as being owned by a charity, the Collegio di Vesta.'

'Gods, you've found them.'

Dressed in hunting clothes and boots, we rode out of Rome in two SUVs on the Via Pontina freeway. Once in the countryside, it dwindled into a standard road, but I was fascinated to see it passed something called the Castrum Legionis.

'It's a re-enactment and education facility for civilians playing at being the ancients, ma'am,' Sergilia looking down her nose with all the superiority of a modern Praetorian. She couldn't see my smile in the fading light. We turned onto the Via Pratica heading for Pratica di Mare, which squatted now on the far more extensive site of old Lavinium. Just past the old castle, we drew into the recess of the Lavinium museum and dropped off half our troops. They disappeared through the hedge and into the trees before we left. They'd have full cover until they reached the gap at the base of the rise the farmhouse stood on.

Conrad had specified one handgun for each detachment leader only plus one for me as we were running a security operation in an allied country. I shuddered at the diplo hassle if the Italian authorities caught us with a load of firearms. In fact, catching us with one would be enough. Being PNG'd would be the least of our worries. We turned at the roundabout as if to go into Pomezia but dived down into a side road. At the end was an empty building plot with a half-rusted sliding gate.

One of Sergilia's troops jumped out and freed the lock, then eased the gate open, careful to make as little noise as possible. The house opposite showed light at the edges of closed shutters at every window. But nosy neighbours were not on tonight's agenda. The SUVs drove in on low revs and parked up behind high untrimmed laurel hedges.

'It's about five hundred metres down into a dip,' Sergilia whispered. 'Open country, but we'd be very unlucky to be spotted. Into the trees, then up the bank and across the top field to target.' She looked at Conrad. 'Your orders, Legate?'

'Your operation, Senior Centurion,' he whispered back. 'You know your troops. Just get me and Major Mitela there and we'll do the political side. *Bona fortuna*.' He grasped her forearm in the traditional salute. She nodded, took two guards with her and melted into the hedgerow. I fingered the little Beretta in my waist holster and wished I had my Glock. We counted a full minute then followed.

Up on the plateau, the farmhouse squatted low with a track leading off northeastwards. The moonlight bleached out the terracotta rooftiles, but not enough to obscure the dim light showing at some windows. We crept forward swinging to the right to follow Sergilia who was aiming for the windowless side of the house. Crouching down in a corner made by the outside wall and an outhouse, I whispered in her ear.

'I'm going to take a look through one of the windows. Stay here.'

She looked as cross as Hades. Tough.

I dropped to my stomach and pulled myself along using my elbows. The nearest window showed no light, but the next one was well lit and I could hear voices through the single glazing. As I stood a few centimetres back from the frame, I brushed against the lower wood sill. Several pieces flaked off followed by a lump. It wasn't a loud noise, but the talking stopped. I dropped back down and stretched out on the ground directly under the window and held my breath. The window latch clunked and I heard the creak of hinges as the window leaves parted inwards. A woman's face peered into the distance, her blonde hair showing white in the moonlight. After a few seconds, the window closed. I released my breath, then crawled back to Conrad and Sergilia.

'The one with the curly blonde hair is here and several others,' I whispered. 'Shall we pay them a call?'

Clutching the Beretta, I flattened myself against the wall by the opening edge of the entrance door. Conrad waited opposite, clutching a heavy rubber torch. Sergilia and four guards stood immobile behind me. I couldn't even hear them breathe.

'One, two three. Go!' I kicked at the door and barrelled in, moving left to let Sergilia in. Her troops spread out and the other detail burst in from the back and surrounded the seven women. Completely immobilised by shock, they stared at us like trapped rabbits. One gave a sob and dropped down onto a chair, covering her face with her hands. I looked at blondie.

'Delfina Balba?' I said.

'What do you want?' she said.

'You to confirm your name for a start.'

She glared at me. 'No.'

'If you're that shy, introduce us to your friends instead.'

'No.'

'Oh dear, there's always one, isn't there? Well, we've identified you personally from the Rome CCTV so no matter.' I turned to Sergilia. 'Have somebody photograph the rest of them and send them for face match. The police will be grateful if we have them all ID'd when we take them in.'

'Who *are* you?' the blonde woman, Balba, asked. 'Not antique dealers.'

'You'd be surprised. Our client is super enthusiastic about her statue and was very disappointed that a crowd of self-appointed imposters stole it.'

Her eyes narrowed. 'What do you mean?'

'You know exactly what I mean. Now where's the statue?'

'Go to hell.'

I nodded at Sergilia. 'Full search, please, and rip anything out you need to.' She flicked her fingers at pairs of guards who hurried off, some clumping up the stairs to the attic space, others outside to the outhouses. I scanned the group of women. 'Sit down all of you, on the floor and leave a metre between each one.'

I raised an eyebrow at Conrad and he nodded.

'This man will take each of you in turn into the kitchen and ask you some questions.' I pointed at the one who sobbed. 'We'll start with her.' She didn't move. Her eyes were wide, terrified. One of the female guards hauled the young woman to her feet and pulled her to the kitchen, followed by Conrad.

'What's he going to do to her?' Balba asked. She sounded anxious. Good.

'She's perfectly safe. However misguided you are, we respect your personal integrity. We just want our property back.'

'You have no right to it,' she cried out and jumped up, fists up. The male *optio* grabbed her shoulder and pushed her back on the ground.

I crossed my arms.

'*You* certainly don't,' I said. 'We bought it from the legal owner. You stole it from us. End of.'

'You know nothing about it.'

'Listen to me, Balba. Whatever centuries-long mission you think you're on, it's too late. It was all over in the 390s when Concordia stepped down as the last *vestalis maxima*. No nostalgic little secret society which can't even keep to decent, let alone pure and noble, behaviour is going to change that. You're done. '

She threw me a nuclear look. I shrugged. After a full minute staring at her, I continued.

'Cloelia of the legend had nothing to do with the vestals in ancient times, let alone now. Meanwhile, there are millions of girls and women out there who could have benefitted from your energy to champion them. Your self-absorbed attitude ignored them and that's the bigger crime.'

'And you completely missed the point, Balba,' Conrad added, guiding the sobbing young woman back from the kitchen. The female Praetorian who'd accompanied them eased her back down onto the floor. 'Vestals kept the honour of Rome, even in the harshest times. You have none. From what your colleague here told me, you now have no purpose.'

The young girl flinched from Balba's incinerating look.

'Your turn,' Conrad said to Balba in a terse voice. 'Come with me.'

She stalked towards the kitchen without looking at him. He and the female Praetorian followed and closed the door quietly behind them.

I stood in silence with the other Praetorians until they returned ten minutes later. Balba looked devastated, but rolled her shoulders back and looked at each of her colleagues one by one. They fixed their eyes on her, but she shook her head. Then she looked away towards the fireplace and released her breath.

Conrad directed his gaze to Sergilia. 'Stop the search now, Senior Centurion. Withdraw all but four guards to the exterior.' Next, he beckoned me to accompany him into the hallway. The guards searching had pulled back a curtain to a storage recess under a beam and scattered its contents. Conrad crouched down and thumped the wall at the side. A panel opened. I hoped it might be a secret passage, but it was a boring cupboard. He stretched in and retrieved the wooden box, still with its silver key in the keyhole. He turned it, opened the bag and there was Cloelia, fixed in silver, but still fleeing Porsena on her horse.

'How the hell did you get her to talk?' I whispered.

'My charming smile,' and he gave a demonstration.

I batted his arm. The smile dropped.

'Be serious,' I said.

'I pointed out the criminal charges she was facing and the harm she was doing to other women. They're not stupid, love, and have a lot to offer if it could be channelled positively.'

'And she believed you?'

'So cynical!'

'I also offered her and her group an expenses paid stay in Roma Nova and time with the pontifex maxima and her staff.'

'Juno. That's pretty generous considering they were beating up on you half the night.'

'Perhaps, but they have very little money and it would be like battering a dying hen. Going after the Cloelia statue was a last fling at convincing themselves of their value and purpose. The pontifex max will give them a good talking to and hopefully convince them their "mission" is over.'

'You think?'

'She may seem a gentle soul on the outside, but underneath she's a bloody determined woman, so yes. The alternative for them is a long stretch here in Italy for assault, kidnapping and theft.' He glanced at me. 'If we can turn them, it will be a better outcome. You never know when we might need a group of allies inside the heart of modern Rome.'

I gasped, and he called me cynical. But I guessed he was only following the ancients' custom of switching enemies into colleagues.

Back in the living room, he turned to Balba.

'Please inform your group what is going to happen to them now.'

We watched the reaction in the women's faces. First, they paid attention, then surprise grew, followed by disbelief. She let them talk it out, then raised her hand to quieten them. I gave her this – she had good control over them.

Conrad called Flavius to book seats on the next Air Roma Nova direct flight for the women; some of Sergilia's detail would accompany them. After collecting their personal belongings, some unfortunately trashed in the search, they stood quietly, if a little forlornly in the living area.

'What happens to us after this trip?' Paola d'Antonio tipped her head up and threw Conrad a hostile look. 'We've been vestals since childhood.'

'Not quite. You took time out to study at university. You have no trainees now, do you? Your college is dying.'

She looked down.

'What you do after your visit to us is entirely up to you,' he replied. 'Perhaps when you see the real way Rome has survived, you may want to stay in Roma Nova. Or perhaps you may agree with Balba and find a new purpose here in modern Rome.'

We took the wooden box with Cloelia and left Sergilia to it. As we marched back across the field, the only sound came from our boots on the soil. I took a deep breath. The evening air was crisp and the moon shone as determinedly as before.

'Supper?' Conrad said. 'I'm sure there's a burger place in the town.'

'Now *you're* kidding *me*,' I replied. I smiled up at him. 'This has been some Roman holiday, Mr Miller.'

He leaned over and kissed me. 'Well, Mrs Miller, to misquote the girl in the film, "in its own way, it's been unforgettable".'

2027

When Carina and Conrad's son, Gillius, nearly blows himself just before the Saturnalia winter holiday, he's sent to Sextilius Gavro, Conrad's 'mad inventor' cousin. Carina is dubious, having met Gavro in New York nearly twenty years before (*INCEPTIO*), but she has no idea how she will be surprised at Saturnalia as a result.

(Set after a few years after SUCCESSIO)

SATURNALIA SURPRISE

Gillius

Gods, she's going to kill me.

    The tile roof I was crouching on started to vibrate. I clung on like a land crab. Smoke wafted up through the rooflight I'd just scrambled through. And the sulphur stink. Down below in the outhouse, the hum grew to a buzz, then a rumble. I covered my ears. Then it all blew.

    A deafening bang. Roar of air. Glass cracked and flew in every direction. It scattered all over the yard. Then silence. My heart pounded like a steam piston. I shivered and not just with the freezing cold of December. The stench of burning wood caught the back of my throat. Hades. Flames leapt through the open rooflight. If I didn't move, I'd burn. I was only thirteen. Not time yet for my funeral pyre.

    People poured out of the back of the house, shouting and pointing. Junia, the steward, leaning on her stick, was holding two of her staff back. The icy yard was covered in shards of glass and broken roof tiles. She clicked her fingers. 'Rakes and brooms, now.' Two of them scurried off. Another two grabbed fire extinguishers. But I saw Dad launch himself at the outhouse door. It gave way under his weight and more smoke billowed out into the freezing air. He ran in, Mama on his heels.

    'No!' I shrieked.

Junia looked up and I froze. She fixed me with such a scathing look, I almost fell off the roof. Dad's voice pierced the roar of the flames. He was shouting my name. I scrabbled to the end of the outhouse roof and peered down in the semi-dark. It was nearly four metres, but the flames were following me along the roof. The heat was toasting my back. I jumped.

I fell into somebody's arms and we landed in a heap on the ground. No breath. My chest spasmed as I dragged in air and retched. Somebody pulled me to my feet. Gods, it was cold. Blood on my knees. People rushing around, shouting, the hiss of the extinguishers and broom bristles scratching as they swept glass. Then my hand was grabbed and almost crushed. I pulled, but the grip tightened. Junia.

'*Domina?*' I heard Junia's voice pierce the haze. 'We've found him. He's safe.'

My mother and father stumbled out of the outhouse door, bent over, coughing and spluttering. Her arms were up over her head to protect her face. Her jeans were scorched and her woollen ripped. He was limping and swearing. I swallowed hard as Mama stopped and fixed me with an ice-blue stare. I lifted my free hand to wave at her, to reassure her. She ran at me and grabbed me to her so tightly I nearly lost my breath again. She drew back. Her face was shiny with sweat and smudged soot. Then she smacked my face, hard.

I sat completely still on the atrium couch, my elbows tucked into my sides, ignoring the throbbing in my hands and arms caused by scrambling over the rough terracotta tiles. I prayed to Mercury to make me invisible. He must have been on a break.

'What the hell do you think you were doing?' Mama glared at me. She was shouting in English. She sometimes lost her Latin when she was cross. Now she was ballistic.

'You're grounded,' she said, 'until I feel like changing my mind.'

I studied the marble floor.

'I'm sorry, Mama.' I looked up. 'I didn't do it on purpose. Give me a break. Please.' I tried my dying fawn look on her.

'Don't try the pathetic routine. You're nearly fourteen, for Chrissakes. Way past that.'

'It was only one more—'

'Don't, Gil. Don't say another word. This is the third time and your luck just ran out.'

'But—'

'No. Go to bed. We'll figure out what to do in the morning.'

I gulped down the last of my honey drink and nearly missed the table when I put my mug down. She looked at me without saying another word; she must have thought I was the dumbest boy in the world. I couldn't move.

I looked at my father. He sat by Mama on the sofa opposite me and was downing a whisky. He was staring out of the tall atrium windows onto the frosty inner courtyard and didn't say a word. His chinos were still covered in smuts. Wrapped round his bare feet were bandages; he'd only been wearing his indoor sandals when he'd run across the shattered window glass in the courtyard. His face was white and hard and wouldn't look at me.

Mama had tears in her eyes, I went to say something, but she just jerked her head at me in an upwards direction, so I trudged off towards the hall and stairs wishing I was an orphan.

Carina

'That was unkind,' I said to Conrad. I went to place my glass on the table and it slipped out of my grip. I just about caught it with my other hand. Junia had slathered too much antiseptic cream over my cut and burnt hands. They weren't so sore now, though.

'I can't bear another ten days of this.' Conrad turned to me. 'We shouldn't have let Helena go off during the school holidays. She's the only one who seems to be able to rein him in.'

'Oh, thanks!'

'I didn't mean it like that.'

'I know.' I reached out and touched his knee. 'She's tutored them since they were babies. She needs regular vacations like anybody else. It's only for a few days and she says she's really serious about this guy.' Of all my cousins, Helena Mitela was the pickiest one I knew. But as a clever and well-connected woman with Vogue-like poise, she could have had anybody. And she'd done exactly that – the glamorous, the intellectual, the political – but they'd all ended badly.

'Well, I hope it works out for her. I don't want to have to go and sort out another no-hoper. Who is he?'

'Not a clue. She's not giving on this one, and I'm not checking him out until she says.'

He rolled his eyes. 'Simple enough for you.'

'Sure, but being the head of the family doesn't mean I'm some kind of licensed buttinsky. She'll tell me when she's ready.'

'Fair enough. But in the meantime, we have to do something about Gil. He causes you so much grief and heartache. I won't have it.'

'He's thirteen. Give him a break,' I said.

'He doesn't give you one. Remember that time he fell off the bridge at the farm in the summer? I watched your face when you saw him lying in a heap on the bank. You looked as if you were dying inside.'

'I thought he must have broken his back or at least his leg. He said he was doing a gravity experiment.' I could smile now at the memory of Gil's earnest explanation as he lay in the hospital bed after we'd taken him to the emergency room. He was surprised that we were stupid with worry about him.

'He doesn't realise the danger he is to himself. Don't they teach them due care at school when they're doing experiments?'

'Of course they do but, Gil says the engineering teacher is a boring fuss-wit who won't let him try new things.'

'Are you defending him?'

'Of course I am.'

'Carina, he's so like you, it's impossible.'

'He looks nothing like me!'

Gil had brown hair and those strange green-brown Tellus eyes that all of Conrad's old family had. Tonia, Gil's twin, was the same. In contrast, I had inherited the dark blue Mitela eyes and red-gold hair from my late grandmother Aurelia.

'Don't prevaricate. You know exactly what I mean.'

I tipped my chin up at him and tried to look stern.

He grinned at me. The hurt and anger drained from his face. He reached along the rolled velvet top of the couch and caught a twist of my hair between his thumb and forefinger.

'Nevertheless, he has to learn boundaries.'

'Sure, but that's part of growing up and he's had a good lesson tonight.'

'You Americans, so soft.' He tweaked my hair.

'I just don't want to crush him. He's so enthusiastic and inventive. Look at that irrigation system he came up with for the upper fields at the farm. But he's driving me crazy. If I don't get this stuff into the Senate president before Saturnalia, she'll have my skin.'

'Why don't we send him to Gavro for a few days?'

'Your mad cousin? You're joking!' While perfectly pleasant, Sextilius Gavro and his mind lived in a different galaxy to everybody else.

'He'd look after Gil, and Gavro's very meticulous. He won't let Gil get away with any sloppiness. They'd be able to work on all sorts of stuff together without bothering other people or anybody bothering them.'

'Exactly. Gil would forget to eat or sleep.'

'Now who's being a fuss-wit?' He smiled at me. 'And don't worry about the domestics. Gavro's got a very efficient housekeeper who keeps him in line. She'll make sure Gil washes his face and brushes his teeth.'

We came down to breakfast next morning and even crossing the atrium, we could hear the shouting. Tonia was in full flow. I stopped and touched Conrad on the arm. He raised an eyebrow and I shook my head.

'I cannot believe I share genes with such an imbecile,' Tonia was screeching.

'At least I don't slobber over some old nag and spend hours shovelling shit,' Gil shouted back.

'No, you just frighten it out of my horse. You've buggered up Saturnalia now. They'll cancel everything and won't let me go to Marcia's party now.'

'They wouldn't anyway – she's a tart.'

The sound of flesh on flesh followed by the crack of a plate shattering as it hit the marble floor.

'Oh, *merda!*' I heard Tonia shriek.

I pushed the door open and was almost knocked over by my daughter hurling herself out of the dining room, tears streaming down her face. Conrad caught her and drew her to him.

'Shhh, come on, dry your eyes. Ten deep breaths.' He handed her a cotton square. He walked her back into the dining room where we found Gil, his hand on his cheek. I pulled it gently away to reveal a bright red patch that was darkening. I shook my head, but smiled at him in sympathy.

'I suggest we all sit down,' Conrad said.

'I don't want—' Tonia said, her voice mutinous.

'Sit down,' I shot back. She flounced to her chair and gave a great sigh as she dropped onto the seat. More emotional than my eldest daughter Allegra, Tonia still had to learn to control those emotions. I fixed her with a hard stare and she dropped her eyes.

'Right, let's go through our ground rules.' I stayed on my feet, crossed my arms and braced my legs. 'One, civilised behaviour at the table. You have not been raised to be barbarians. Two, no fighting, physical or verbal abuse. You should have grown out of that at five. I just heard a scene I thought would never happen in my house. And third, when your father asks you to do something, you do it.' I looked at Tonia who had dropped her head. Her curling hair fell in ripples like mini waterfalls either side of her face. 'Look at me, Antonia.' Her face appeared. 'Do you understand?'

'Yes, Mama,' she mumbled.

'Gillius?'

'Yes, Mama.' He looked mortified.

'Good, now somebody pour me some coffee. I'm tired already.'

Conrad called Sextilius Gavro after breakfast to ask the favour, but his cousin was strangely reticent, even when Conrad invited him to spend the whole Saturnalia holiday with us afterward. He asked Conrad to hold for a moment, blanked the screen. We could hear muffled speech in the distance. After half a minute, Gavro returned to the screen and said he would love to have Gil stay as his 'sorcerer's apprentice'.

'That almost sounds like a joke,' I said as Conrad closed the phone terminal. 'Is Gavro feeling all right?'

'He's not as dry as you think, Carina. I thought he'd come out of his shell when I saw him a couple of months ago. Perhaps he's developing a sense of humour as he gets older.'

'How old is he exactly?'

'What a question! He's three years younger than me.'

'Forty-seven? Juno! Then he can only have been thirty, no, twenty-nine when he walked into my New York office with you. He seemed middle-aged even then.'

I helped Gil pack for a week's visit.

'You know Uncle Gavro. He stayed overnight with us when he had some business in the city about a year ago.'

'He's okay, but a bit weird,' Gil looked up at me as I put an extra woollen in his case.

'Weird how?'

'He kept talking to himself whenever he thought nobody was listening.'

I frowned as I remembered Gavro jotting figures and calculations in a notebook and doodling drawings at the table. He'd apologised, embarrassed, but resumed when the next thought entered his overactive brain.

'But he *was* interesting when I talked to him,' Gil admitted. 'And he was okay listening to some of my ideas.' He looked up at me. 'But I really don't want to go, Mama. I have a special project I want to finish before Saturnalia and I haven't got much time. I promise I'll be good. I'll work quietly in my bedroom. Please.'

'You'll be able to work on all sorts of stuff with Gavro,' I said as firmly as I could in the face of Gil's best efforts. 'He has a completely fitted out workshop. You won't bother other people, and nobody will bother you.'

'I still don't want to go,' Gil muttered.

We drove east on the Brancadorum road for ten kilometres. Gavro mostly stayed in his house in the middle of nowhere. His mother had been a professor of control mechanics and an old university friend as well as cousin of Conrad's mother, Constantia, but Gavro hadn't taken to the academic life.

His short figure appeared as soon as we rang the doorbell. His brown hair was combed neatly, his dark brown pants were clean and pressed, and he wore an open neck shirt under a taupe jersey. Gone was the scruffy inventor in a smeared and dull coverall. But he still twitched with nervous energy.

'Carina, Conrad, welcome. Come in, come in. Don't let's heat the whole of Brancadorum!'

Another joke.

'Ah, and here's my temporary apprentice,' he said. 'Let me have a proper look at you, young man.'

'Close your mouth,' Conrad whispered to me as Gil was answering Gavro's questions, nervously at first, then becoming more confident. Soon, Conrad and I were forgotten as Gavro and Gil were firing questions and answers at each other, both leaning forward, eager in their conversation.

'Told you he'd changed,' Conrad whispered to me as we left.

A week after we'd taken Gil to Gavro's the Saturnalia preparations were nearly complete under Junia's supervision; her last. She was retiring after the January Agonalia. Her back injuries during the Great Rebellion had finally caught up with her. I sent her to the best orthopaedic consultant at the Central Valetudinarium, but at seventy-two she had to accept defeat. I saw her more than once slip a couple of painkillers in her mouth when she was sitting in an easy chair, cushions packed under and round her. Her son, Macrinus, the new under-steward, was directing the servants. He'd become her 'legs' in the past few months.

A huge mesh-sided hand truck brimming with greenery was parked in the middle of the atrium. A cold blast blew through the gap where they hadn't quite closed the atrium glass sliding door when they'd wheeled it in.

I shivered. Junia spotted it and flicked her fingers at one of the juniors who scurried to close the panel. Gods, she missed nothing.

'*Domina.*' She gave a tiny bow of her head and tried to rise, but I waved her back down and sat with her.

'I see you have it all under control as usual, Junia,' I said. 'Congratulations.' I looked through the sliding doors at the sky full of grey rolls of cloud. 'Snow this evening, do you think?'

'Yes, and the forecast is for several days of heavy fall. When is Gillius due back?'

She knew perfectly well he was coming home in two days' time, but was courteous enough to ask.

'Thursday, but I don't think there'll be a problem – they'll keep the main Brancadorum road clear.'

My main concern was that Gil would forget what day it was. I wasn't too sure Gavro would remember either to join us for the meal on the seventeenth.

Gillius

Gavro made me phone home after the third day. I was right at a critical point in testing my project. He'd given me my own bench area and computer and shown me the racks of tools, materials, and test equipment. It was Elysium. He said I could use any chemicals and metals, but I had to ask first and write it all down in the record book. He made me keep proper lab notes just like at school, but he didn't hover or fuss.

'Gil? How are you doing?' Mama asked. 'Not getting in Gavro's way?'

'No, course not. He's been brilliant. We've worked on loads of stuff.' I showed her my model for a portable bridge and a prototype for a low-tech vehicle. I was embarrassed at the communicator; it worked, but the case was crude and didn't fit, but I'd fix that. I looked at her face. Her smile widened. 'And I'm working on something really special, Mama. I can't wait to show you.'

'Well, these look pretty special to me, Gil.'

'No, much better, you'll see!'

'Everything else okay? You *are* remembering to wash?'

'Gods, Mama, I'm not some kid. Anyway, Gavro's, er, friend reminds me.'

'Friend? He has a friend there as well? Who is it?'

I looked her directly in the eyes.

'Oh, nobody special. Just a guest for a few days, Gavros says. They don't bother us, though.'

'Well, mind your manners.'

I rolled my eyes at her. She'd never guess.

After lunch the next day, it started to snow. I clicked on the screen for the weather link. Days of it. Great. Snowball fight with Tonia. She'd just squeal. I glanced at the date. Hades. Today was the fifteenth. We had to get back home tomorrow for Saturnalia the day after. Gavro had a four-wheel drive, so we'd be fine. And they were bound to clear the main road.

'Are you okay, Gil? And Uncle Gavro?' Mama's face in the screen looked worried.

'We're fine,' I replied. 'We're blocked in, but Uncle Gavro says the *curia* at Brancadorum is bound to clear and grit the main road to the city. It'll be okay, Mama as long as it doesn't snow again, he says.'

She closed her eyes for a moment.

Then the signal failed. We'd lost screen-to-screen comms.

I got her back on audio.

'Don't take any risks tomorrow, will you, darling? Tell Uncle Gavro—'

The signal cut, permanently this time.

Carina

We were snowed in. The newsies were having a field day with their graphs and charts. The ploughs and tractors were out soon enough despite it being an official holiday and the main city roads including ours were cleared. Although many of the public Saturnalia celebrations were cancelled, the priests would make the usual grand sacrifice and invoke Saturn's blessings. I pitied them today; it was a Greek rite and they'd have to shiver in sleeveless fringed tunics with heads bare instead of a warm wool toga snugly draped over the head. It was a sure bet they'd turn up the heating in the Temple of Saturn and have every open brazier burning hard.

Brancadorum was cut off and we'd lost screen-to-screen communications with Gavro during the incessant snowfall. Even the satellite phones wouldn't work because of signal attenuation.

'I don't know when it'll stop,' Conrad said looking out at the bleak, grey sky through the flakes. 'I think I'll go and check the old HF radio in the basement.'

'I thought you'd gotten rid of that. Isn't it steam-driven?'

'No sarcasm, thank you. It may be old, but it'll get through this lot. The problem is, I don't know if Gavro still has a set.'

He and Macrinus lugged the black-and-grey-cased relic upstairs and Conrad started fiddling with cables.

'I'll just go and set up the antennae.'

I watched from the back sitting room which had been knocked

through to the old *triclinium* to provide a sunroom giving on to a terrace. He and Macrinus were out in the snow attaching wire to pre-positioned hooks that had been used in my grandmother's day after the Great Rebellion. Then, transport and telephone infrastructure had been damaged and they'd found it more reliable to use field signal equipment for a few months to maintain basic communications.

Although my grandmother had updated the equipment about twenty years ago, it was still pretty crude, requiring tens of metres of cable to form an antenna. And this wasn't the weather to be trudging around in fixing it.

I thrust hot brandy and honey drinks at Conrad and Macrinus as they came in through the kitchen service door and stamped their boots on the mat. They pulled their hats off and unwound the scarves protecting their faces, showering snow over the scullery area.

'Thanks, love,' Conrad said. 'It's enough to freeze Mars' balls off out there. And it doesn't look as if it's going to let up.'

He hunched over the set, fiddling around trying to get a signal, but we only heard atmospherics and other people's garbage. In his thirty-year Praetorian career, he'd used every kind of communications equipment, so no amateur. But he gave up around midnight.

The next morning it was still snowing, but nowhere near the blizzard of the previous evening.

'Well, we're not going to see Gil here for tomorrow. That really sucks,' I said to nobody in particular. Conrad was reading his periodical, Tonia her book. She looked up and gave me a little smile. Then the radio crackled.

'Calling Mitela. Hello, Mitela.'

Gil.

Conrad leapt up and grabbed the handset.

'Mitela. Go ahead.'

'*Salve*, Dad. It's me!'

'Are you okay, Gil? And Uncle Gavro?'

'We're good. We're snowed in at the moment but once the *curia* at Brancadorum sends that tractor out, the road'll be clear.'

I closed my eyes in relief they were safe.

'Has Gavro spoken to the *curia* highways people himself?' Conrad said.

'Not exactly...'

'What do you mean?'

'His landline is stuffed, and my phone can't get a signal, but he says they usually come out so not to worry.'

I glared at the old transceiver. How could Gil be so nonchalant? And Gavro?

'I wasn't sure Gavro had an old radio,' Conrad said quickly after he glanced my face.

'He didn't, but I've built him one now,' Gil continued. 'It was all I could think of. And he told me what frequencies to try.'

I could hear the grin in his voice.

'Well done, Gil. Very well done.' Conrad nearly choked. 'Here, talk to your mother.' He pushed the handset at me.

'Give us an update before you set off. Don't take any risks tomorrow, will you? Tell Uncle Gavro the same.'

'Don't worry, Mama, we'll be careful. I know I'm not supposed to tell, but you'll never guess—'

His voice cut. Conrad pressed buttons, flicked switches – nothing but static.

'Damn. It must be their end,' he said. 'We don't know what they were using.'

'A lot of ingenuity, components and copper wire put together by a kid with a soldering iron,' I replied. 'Gods, I'm so proud of him. But what if it snows again overnight?'

The three of us sat in silence at breakfast on the seventeenth. Bright sunshine flooded the room; it had stopped snowing at last. Our eldest, Allegra, although a very junior officer, been drafted in with the rest of the military to help ensure vital services were kept running. She'd called first thing to say she should be able to join us just after two when she finished her shift.

'I'll be there, Mama, as long as there are no further disturbances in the city.'

'What do you mean, "disturbances"?'

'Unfortunately,' she said in the driest tone I'd ever heard her use, 'some people seem to think the *custodes* concentrating on the bad weather crisis means they can help themselves to what's in the shops. I've been freezing my, er, extremities off in the Macellum district all night. We came across some kids with a crowbar in front of a smashed window, pulling stuff out of an electrical goods shop. The alarm was going, so were others all up the street. As soon as they saw us, though, they ran like the Furies were after them.' She chuckled.

The sight of half a dozen Praetorians marching towards you with intent and attitude would make anybody run.

'But they've managed to open the basilica after all for the public banquet. My oppo, Sergilia, has caught guard duty there,' she added.

After checking last details with Macrinus for the celebratory meal later, I retreated to my office for an hour to check nobody had found my stash of gifts for the twenty-third. Sigillaria was important not just for the kids who loved new toys, but when adults gave each other something to compensate for the excesses that would happen today.

Normally on Saturnalia morning, Helena and I would sip a glass of champagne and exchange jokes and snippets of gossip. She had more than a finger on the pulse of city life; its lifeblood ran through her. She'd also forewarn me about any particularly risqué activities the household staff were planning for today. Ceding my place at the head of the Mitela tribe for a day to the *princeps Saturnalicius* was all well and good, but even misrule and chaos had its limit as far as I was concerned. Helena would also make sure the children were safely out of the way when the horseplay became a little raunchy. I hadn't heard from her, but presumed she'd make it back for today.

Conrad tried to contact Gavro again, but no answer on the radio, nor were digital communications back up yet. As I trudged upstairs to change into my over-bright turquoise Saturnalia tunic ready to greet any guests who would manage to get here, I realised this would be the first time without all the children here – a pretty depressing thought.

Gillius

Gavro said nothing at breakfast the next morning, but kept looking outside.

'I'll go and check the car in a minute,' he said. 'Best we start early. Everything packed?'

I nodded. My special project was safe in my backpack. I'd put my walking boots on and warmest sweater plus some of Gavro's mountain walking trousers. He'd insisted on giving me a stupid bobble hat with strings to tie under the chin. No way was I going to wear the stripey horror. Tonia would die laughing if she saw me in it. I stuffed it in my parka pocket.

I stood in the vestibule of the closed down house. Gavro's housekeeper had left for her sister's in Brancadorum in her four-by-four yesterday. It was only a short distance, so she could probably walk it if she was stuck. Gavro's guest, whose identity I was bursting to reveal to Mama, had gone to see her friend there yesterday and would come back to travel with us to the city for Saturnalia. To be honest, I was relieved to have a break. It was too embarrassing when she and Gavro snogged when they thought nobody was looking.

The heating was off, the shutters closed. It was eerily quiet. Where the hell was Gavro? He must have been gone over ten minutes. I went out, leaving the door on the latch. The snow was piled up on both sides. Gavro had gone out last night in the freezing cold to clear it from the drive. I could see his footprints set in ice.

'Uncle Gavro? Are you there?' I called out as I pushed open the garage door.

No reply.

The car was there, big black and shiny, but no Gavro.

A low moan came from the other side of the car. Gods, that was scary!

'Wh— who's there?' I said.

'Gil. It's me.'

Gavro. How stupid was I? Of course, it could only be him.

'Where are you?'

'By my door. I've had a fall.'

The *custodes* arrived in a half-tracked vehicle twenty-eight minutes after I'd called them. The paramedics bent over Gavro and fixed plastic supports all the way up his arm. As they wheeled him on a trolley into the back of the vehicle, he reached out and seized my hand. 'Tell Carina I'm so sorry.'

'Don't worry, Uncle Gavro. She'll be fine. I mean, she'll be really sorry you're in hospital for Saturnalia and won't be able to be with us.'

'No, you don't understand. You won't be able to go home now.'

His hand released mine and dropped down. He closed his eyes. The *custos* closed the vehicle doors. She turned to me. 'Now, young man, we're taking Sextilius Gavro straight to the polyclinic in Brancadorum, then we'll be back for you. My colleague is going to stay here with you while I arrange a bed for you. We'll let your mother know over the military net where you are.'

'But I'm going home, back to the city.'

'Not a prayer. The road's treacherous and blocked in several places. They're trying to clear it, but it won't be until after Saturnalia now.' She smiled at me. 'You wouldn't have got through anyway.'

'Can't I go on the train?'

'It's only on a skeleton service today and many of the lines are iced-up. Most of the phone lines are down as well.' She frowned at me. 'Sorry, son, I'm not letting a juvenile go off by himself in these conditions and that's flat.'

I stared at her. Not be at home for Saturnalia? After all my work? She was joking. She creased her face and gave me a stern look. While the other *custos* and I waited at the house, I tried to call home via the old radio, but it wouldn't connect. Maybe one of the transistors had died.

I hunched in a chair in the cold living room and wiped a tear from my eye before the *custos* sitting opposite could spot it. Saturnalia was completely stuffed now. All my work down the pan. And I wouldn't see Mama's face when she opened it. I sniffed. Hard.

Somebody was banging at the door. The *custos* jerked his head up, then pulled himself out of his chair. His colleague must be back to take me to strangers. But nobody was more surprised than me to see Gavro's 'guest'. How had she got back from her friend's in Brancadorum? She was dressed in a red winter parka, a furry hat on her head, and red walking boots. She removed her sunglasses as she paused in the living room door entrance.

'Where's Sextilius? And why is there a *custos* here?'

After he'd explained, she gave him her dazzling smile and told him she would take over. She had to sign something, then bundled me into her four-by-four parked outside.

'Right. First stop Brancadorum Valetudinarium to collect Sextilius, then we hack our way into the city.'

'But suppose we can't get through?'

'Your great grandmother Aurelia said there's no such word as "can't", only "won't".'

Carina

By early afternoon the atrium blazed with light. Everywhere was covered in ferns, spruce and pine. And in the centre was a large square table covered with linen, silverware, glasses, candles and the best china. I smelt roast pork, lemons and spices. In tune with the reversal of the day, Junia was enthroned in my usual place, Macrinus beside her. Conrad handed me a glass of champagne. He was on waiter duty. His Saturnalia tunic was bright orange. He shrugged, then grinned. Wearing over-colourful clothes was traditional, but a strain on the eyes.

'It's only for a day,' he whispered.

'I know, but I wish Gil was here. And Allegra hasn't arrived.'

'Well, Tonia's having fun.' He pointed to her skipping between people with trays of hors d'oeuvres, watched anxiously by Macrinus. I could see at least one of the trays coming to grief, contents slithering across the marble floor.

'Io Saturnalia!'

I blinked at the hearty shout from the household and guests gathered around and raised my glass, then bowed towards Junia. She went to speak, but a blast of cold air and a loud thud interrupted her. All heads turned towards the atrium doors, now open. Allegra, in her fatigues and winter parka, cheeks burning with the indoor heat, tore off her field cap and shouted, 'Io Saturnalia!'

They shouted back, the noise filling the atrium. I hugged her to me, ignoring the cold and wet of her thick coat.

'I've brought you something else, Mama,' she whispered in my ear and nodded towards the double doors. On the threshold stood a group; a lanky boy – Gil – and a man with an arm strapped up, his figure muffled in a thick coat, scarf and hat – Sextilius Gavro. But I nearly stopped breathing when I saw the woman with her arm through Gavro's sound one. It was my cousin Helena. She was looking at Gavro as if there was nobody else in the room.

'I wanted to tell you, Mama,' Gil said into my ear as I hugged him. 'But she swore me to secrecy. Then the radio blew up and Uncle Gavro didn't have any more transistors.' He glanced round to see if anybody was near. 'They're a bit soppy, but they behave properly most of the time.'

I chewed my lips to keep my grin inside my mouth; Helena and 'proper' didn't connect in my mind. She broke off looking at Gavro for a second to grin at me. Then she blushed and resumed Gavro adoration.

'I've brought you something special,' Gil pulled me out of my stunned state. 'I know it's not the twenty-third yet, but I wanted you to have it now on the table instead of a boring old candle.' He rummaged in his bag and pulled out what looked like a pair of terracotta bowls, one inverted on top of the other and securely tied together. He hugged them to his middle in one hand and pulled me to my place on the table with the other. He placed them on the table and cut the ties.

'I wanted to say sorry again about blowing up the outhouse, but I was trying to make this.'

I reached out and put my arm around his shoulder and kissed him. 'I've forgiven you long ago about that.'

He grinned at me, so like his father's, and removed the top bowl. A pale yellow glow was reflected in the glazed interior, then it grew in intensity to almost white. People nearby stopped talking and stared. A tiny pop, almost a sigh, came from the bowl and the room was flooded with light. Red chased yellow, blue and violet around the room as the light flickered, orange and green mixing and blending. It was the most beautiful thing I had seen.

No, that was my unruly son's face.

Io Saturnalia, indeed!

2029

Highly intelligent, efficient and dedicated to her career in the military, Carina and Conrad's eldest daughter, Allegra, is losing her grip on her life. Her introverted character prevents her from acknowledging her feelings for a man she has known all her life, let alone doing anything about it.

Macrinus, the under-steward, has grown up in the Mitela household. His mother was a comrade-in-arms of Aurelia Mitela during the Great Rebellion and has told him Allegra is out of his reach.

(Set several years after SUCCESSIO)

ALLEGRA AND MACRINUS

Macrinus

'Hey, Macrinus.'

Allegra. She was the only one who remembered all the time. Even now some of the household still called me by my childhood name, Macro. I hated it. The school bully had called me "Micro-Macro" and the others had taken it up, chanting round me in a circle. I hadn't run as I'd wanted too, but I'd prayed to Pluto to pull me down to Tartarus where I could disappear and hide for eternity in a quiet dark corner.

But Allegra never forgot. And she always gave me a smile – the twin of her mother's – wide, full teeth. It spread up into her eyes and lit up her whole serious face.

I can't remember exactly when Allegra slid from being my little friend, happily chattering away, asking questions, eating honey cake in the kitchen with my mother fondly watching her, into a young woman. She'd been an awkward slope-shouldered teenager, almost grumpy, when I went away to London. Maybe it was her dad's illness and the trials, but when I returned she'd grown up.

I'd walked through the vestibule late evening, tired after the flight from London and my leaving party the night before. The fading daylight through the large side windows lit the atrium just enough not to bother switching the light on. I'd been desperate for a shower followed by a cold beer. But before I'd reached the domestic hall entrance a figure had sprung up from the huddle by the sliding glass doors to the inner courtyard.

Allegra.

She must have been waiting for me. Her face had been half in shadow, half pink and gold from the evening light. Neither of us had said anything. She'd just stared at me.

'Welcome home, Macrinus,' she'd said eventually in a low voice just a level above a whisper. I'd seen the flush in her face, even in the dim light as she'd tipped her chin up. Before I'd been able to reply, she'd turned and fled.

That was three years ago. Now she stood there in her military fatigues, tall, assured and confident at nineteen, head tipped to one side. You could almost see the ghosts of generations of Roman warriors behind her. She gave me a slight frown.

'What's up? You look like you've swallowed a sour olive. Or maybe a jarful.'

'No, nothing, *domina*, thank you.'

Her face tightened into a fierce frown, anger bursting from her eyes.

'Do not ever, ever, call me that.'

She actually stamped her foot clad in its field boot on the marble floor. The studs screeched. Another, more logical part of my mind made a note to get one of the juniors to polish out the scratches in the morning.

She'd always been 'Allegra' to me. When you're sixteen and a six-year-old follows you around, you call her by her name. When she's sixteen and becomes the heir to the senior of the Twelve Families of Roma Nova and I'm the steward's child, I knew I had to step back and give her the respect of her position. My mother would have flayed me alive if I hadn't. Ma might be retired now, living in the garden annex, but she heard about everything and could still bite as if she was running the place.

Allegra's frown deepened, contorting her face. She flushed, stared at me for a few moments, then stalked off, her back as straight as if she was on a parade.

I had no doubt offended her, but I couldn't let my guard slip. Besides, I was a good ten years older than her. She'd partner or even marry some senator's son, produce the next Mitela family heir and I'd have to get on with my life.

But it was getting worse each time I saw her. I closed my eyes and took a deep breath. Thank Mars she was away training most of the time.

Five minutes later when the stillness of the marble columns and pale stone walls had calmed me, I made my way down the corridor to my office. I couldn't face going through the accounts yet again with old Galienus now. The Censor's officer was conducting an inspection into us this coming week and Galienus was panicking. All our figures were up to date and every required legal and tax return filed in full and on time. We'd plenty of time to prepare, but the basic problem was he insisted on using software he'd introduced over three years ago when it was already half obsolete. If only he trusted me to update the system. But the Styx would dry up before he agreed to let me install anything new.

What was the use of my three years at the Central University and an MBA from London, the world's financial centre, if I couldn't use it? But Galienus regarded anything I wanted to change with deep suspicion. He was the steward so I had to buckle down even though I was itching to put my skills to use. Ma said I should wait; he was bound to retire soon. He could hardly see beyond his spectacles.

Back in the domestic office, I slumped in front of my screen and poked at the keyboard. Hades take them all. I tapped in a number and called Marcus.

The next day, the marble floor of the atrium reflected the morning sun particularly harshly. The Furies were hammering on the inside of my skull with their brass-studded scourges. But it had been a great evening with Marcus and the two girls. Mine had been lovely; charming, a superb dancer, non-giggler and a great lover. I was about to ask her out again, just the two of us, over breakfast when Marcus had whispered she was a *hetaera*. Gods, I could have smacked his smirk through his head and out the other side.

'What the hell were you playing at?' I spat at him.

'You looked as if you needed some major cheering up.' He grinned at me. 'Only the best would have done. Seems to have worked. She's looking for a new permanent client. You could do worse.'

I was appalled, not at the girl – she must have been embarrassed enough at dealing with such an amateur like me – but bloody Marcus. He was one of those hard-working, hard-living, hard-drinking types but his clever eyes missed nothing. Did he think I needed to hire a companion? That I couldn't go out and find somebody if I wanted?

'Come on, man, you can't keep wasting your time over The Impossible One. Either pounce or leave. If you don't, you'll find yourself sitting in the forum with all the other old crumblies trying to remember the last time you had a shag.'

Perhaps Marcus was right. I stared at the leaves in the enormous planter in the centre of the atrium right under the oculus, the bull's-eye in the roof. I'd cut myself on the exotic sword-shaped leaves when running too close to them so many times as a kid. The little cut marks appeared a little further down my arm each year until I'd learnt to avoid such an obvious danger.

Nothing would induce me to 'pounce', so I had no other choice but to update my CV. Gods, that was a depressing thought. I pulled my shoulders up; I'd start this afternoon. It would be painful, a wrench. Apart from the two years in London, Domus Mitelarum had been my home all my life. My mother had never said a word about my father, even when I was emancipated at sixteen. She'd been forty-three when she fell pregnant, ten years after the rebellion. I couldn't imagine who it could have been. Like any child I found the thought of my parent having sex embarrassing. It's just not how you see them.

Ma had always seemed a heroic figure, loyally supporting old Countess Aurelia, both in the military and back here afterwards. And when Ma was running the household and businesses, nothing was a hair's width out of perfect order. Nor anyone.

But for me, she was my comfort, my haven, the person I loved most in the world. When I came home from school, she'd wipe my grubby face, sit me down with milk and a sandwich, comfort my worries and listen to my triumphs. She had all the time in the world for me. It was only as I grew older that I realised she had ring-fenced certain times and wouldn't tolerate any interruption during that precious hour or later when she read with me at bedtime.

When I was seventeen, she told me that if I passed the entrance exam, I would go to the Central University the following year at the old countess's expense. Joining the household and working there like any other junior when I wasn't studying seemed a small price to pay. Unlike many students I had a warm home, plenty to eat, beer money from my wages and access to one of the best private libraries and state of the art computer systems. Ma even gave me an old car to go out with. Life couldn't have been more perfect.

Three years after graduation, and with the hint of becoming Galienus's deputy, I went off to London to work in Soanes, a big City firm that old Countess Aurelia had some connections to and studied for my MBA. Ma retired when I came back full of big ideas and I slid into the number two slot under Galienus, her former deputy. He'd been there man and boy and loved the whole household machine; the family, the servants, cousins, famous guests, events, crises and household secrets. Of course, they made up an integral part of the Mitela family. Roma Novans considered the whole household from top to bottom as an organic entity, each member with their own duties and responsibilities, from the countess down to the groundsman's boy. After the sophistication of London it all seemed a little quaint, but it worked.

After a few months, Galienus had handed oversight of the Mitela business interests to me, so that was something. To be honest, I didn't think he'd been particularly interested, but had carried out the necessary work on them because it was his duty. Managing the businesses and investments gave me a buzz. As well as closing local deals, I travelled business class twice a year to the EUS to visit Brown Industries which has been founded by Countess Carina's American father. Maybe I could sound out my contacts there for an opening. There was, of course, the Pulcheria Foundation. Allegra's mother was strangely reluctant to part with her shares in it. Hidden behind a dark glass facade in the financial quarter of the city here in Roma Nova, it was smooth, efficient and very profitable; their CEO had won Businesswoman of the Year last year. But I always had the feeling of being watched when I went to the shareholder meetings; there was some mystery there. I wouldn't be sending my CV to them.

Absorbed in those half-happy, half-sad thoughts, I hardly noticed what was going on around me as I crossed the atrium to the steward's office. My next objectives were analgesics for my head and a large mug of hot black coffee.

'Look where you're going, you idiot.'

I looked down and saw an overall-clad figure, hair plaited and pinned, and crouching down, one arm stretched underneath the coffee table, a duster in her hand. A plastic tote with sprays, sponges and hand brush was on the floor, millimetres in front of my foot. My reprimand for such a cheeky, no, downright rude, comment from a junior domestic was ready to shoot off my tongue, but as I opened my mouth my brain registered the voice. My hangover must be worse than I thought. I kept seeing and hearing Allegra everywhere. My priority had to be getting out of this house.

The figure looked up and sto*od* up in one fluid movement.

Gods. It *was* Allegra.

She glanced at me, then fixed her gaze through the large glass sliding doors into the courtyard garden behind me. The colour in her face grew from a delicate pink to full flush, as if she'd been caught pilfering the family treasure account.

'Go on, say it,' she said. 'Everybody else has.'

She looked drained and miserable. Her shoulders drooped, and she fidgeted with the duster.

'Here, give that to me,' I said and snatched it out of her hand. 'Sit down while I go and find out what the hell is going on. You shouldn't have to be cleaning something yourself. I'll get somebody on it straight away.'

'No, you don't understand.' She brought her hand up to flick an escaped strand of hair back.

'No, I don't. Where the hell is the housekeeper?'

Allegra put her hand out and touched my forearm to stop me striding off to the domestic hall. A tingle like electricity shot up my arm. I just about stopped myself gasping, but took a long breath instead, praying she hadn't noticed my reaction.

'Don't tell me you haven't heard?' she said. 'You must be the only one who hasn't.' She tipped her head up in her usual way. Much better.

'What? I had a late start this morning.'

'Oh, I suppose that's why you weren't there this morning for the briefing.'

The housekeeper gathered the staff together at seven thirty every morning over a cup of coffee to give them their tasks, and any news. I usually attended, but not every time.

'What's happened, Allegra?'

She burst into tears.

I wanted to do nothing else but pull her into my arms, hold her while she cried, and comfort her. Instead, I led her to one of the sofas, my hand cupping her elbow. I released it reluctantly and fetched her a glass of water from the tray on the side table. I nearly gulped it down myself. But she needed her friend, not some trembly-handed infatuated boy.

She crouched on the edge of the sofa.

'I've been grounded, suspended for a week.' Her voice was so low I wasn't sure I'd heard her. 'They chucked me out of the Praetorian building. I wasn't even allowed to collect my things.'

'Why?'

'Insubordination, supposedly. But it wasn't.' Her head came up with a jerk. 'I merely pointed something out to Major Fausta and she told me I was wrong. I wasn't. My friend Diana Sergilia was shaking her head at me to let it go, but I thought the major really ought to know, so I repeated it and Fausta told me to can it. I tried again, very politely, to explain, but she turned round and came down hard on me, then suspended me for a week. I was marched out of the building and left on the street.'

'Surely they can't do that?' I knew the Praetorians were tough, but that seemed harsh. I wanted to find this major and tell her what I thought of her.

'Of course they can.' She gave a short brittle laugh. 'Don't worry, Macrinus, I could survive anywhere, let alone a really easy place like the city. I was going to go to a friend's and lie low for the week, then I thought it through. Fausta was bound to call my mother – they're friends and worked together for years.'

'Countess Carina would understand, though. I heard she used to get into trouble herself.'

Allegra snorted. Not a refined noise.

'Don't you believe it. She was furious and has put me on chores all this week, which is why I'm here.'

'You can't work as a servant in your own house.'

'Huh. Apparently, that's what they do in America. Badly behaved children have to do extra chores around their house.'

'But you're not a child—'

'No, but you tell me what choice I have.' She looked out of the wide patio doors, her mouth not drooping, but set in a tight line I'd rarely seen.

I was so angry on Allegra's behalf. She was tough, no doubt, and three years' hard training had given her skills and confidence, but she had one vulnerability. When she thought she was right, she wouldn't let it go. The problem for others was she was nearly always right.

Countess Carina was friendly and businesslike at our regular oversight meeting that afternoon. Some of her witty remarks passed Galienus by; he took every word she said so seriously. She glanced at me several times as I often smiled at her jokes, but I couldn't today. Nor could I look at her as I gave the latest status report. She was no different from usual but I couldn't help seeing her in a changed light. She'd acted harshly, deliberately putting her daughter into a humiliating position. How could she have done that?

At last, the meeting ended. Galienus gathered up his el-pad and file of papers and scuttled off. The countess stayed in her seat. I bowed and went to follow Galienus out.

'One moment, Macrinus.'

'*Domina*?'

'Sit down. Please.'

She'd used my formal name.

'Okay, what's the problem?' she said.

'I'm sorry, I don't understand. Was there something wrong in my presentation?'

'Don't use that passive-aggressive snotty tone with me, young man. I've seen it all.' Her voice was noticeably cooler. She fixed her gaze on me. It was like being lasered by blue light.

'I apologise, *domina*, but it's nothing.'

'Nothing? I don't think so. Not when you've sat poker-faced through an informal meeting, speaking as if live coals were dragging each word out of your mouth.'

I said nothing. If I started, I wasn't sure I would be able to stop.

'C'mon, Macro, maybe I can help?'

I shook my head.

'Are you okay here? Still happy to work as Galienus's number two or is he driving you completely crazy?' She rubbed her fingers along the length of her el-pad stylus, then laid it down on the table. 'Entirely confidentially, he'll be gone in the next twelve months. He's a lovely guy and one of my oldest friends, but I think he'll be happy to retire.'

'I, too, am thinking about my future but there's so much to consider.'

She gave me a long, cool look.

'Well, be sure to let me know of your plans in good time. I'd be lost without your common sense. And you knock on my door if you want to talk anything over. Anything.'

I logged off just after seven and thought I'd drop in to see Ma before I ate. Her flat was two rooms, kitchen and bathroom with an outside courtyard. It was screened from the main house by half-height stone wall and a trellis covered in honeysuckle, but her view was over the garden that stretched to a mini parkland behind Domus Mitelarum.

She was seventy-four, not a great age for a Roma Novan, but her back injuries during the rebellion had incapacitated her early. I was sure she'd disliked stepping down from being steward, but equally sure that her body was relieved when the stress of the day-to-day management of such a complex household and associated businesses had stopped. Galienus still took problems to her and asked for her advice and I know Countess Carina often stopped by for a quiet chat.

I bent down and kissed Ma's cheek. She brought her hand up to my face and stroked it and smiled. We sat in the warm sun on the teak chairs, well padded, she drinking her old lady port and me a Castra Lucillan red.

After a few minutes' relaxing silence she said, almost casually, 'Tell me.'

'I'm just a bit tired. You know we've got the Censor's officer visit next week. Gally's driving me insane with all his wittering.' I gave her a smile. She didn't comment, but sipped her drink. By the time she'd finished, the sun was hovering like an orange incandescent ball on the horizon and flooded the garden with deep yellow light.

'Now tell me the truth,' she said.

'It's Allegra.'

'Ah.'

'I was so angry to find her dressed as a junior skivvy wiping dust off the furniture. What in Hades was her mother thinking of? It'll unsettle the staff and it's so humiliating for her.'

'Well, it's unsettled you,' Ma replied tartly.

'It's not me I'm worried about.'

'No?'

I finished my glass, but said nothing.

'Countess Carina is often unorthodox,' my mother said. 'As you would expect, she's kept some of her American ideas. This is one of them. It's not such a bad one, either.'

'You can't possibly agree.'

'Don't be ridiculous, Macro. You know perfectly well that an efficient household runs on good discipline. Allegra works in a very structured environment. She knows what rules mean. If she's broken them, she has to pay.' She smiled at me. 'You've always been sensitive around her, protecting her. You have to let go and let her fight her own battles. She's done it before, you know.'

I shrugged. 'It won't be a problem much longer,' I said. 'I'm thinking of leaving.'

'What?' She looked appalled, as if I'd broken every law in the Twelve Tables. 'Why on earth would you want to leave? You seemed so pleased to come home after London. You said you never wanted to go away again.'

'I need a change.'

She turned her whole body round and fixed me with a hard stare. I kept looking forward.

'Why aren't you telling me the truth, Macro?'

'I just need to get away, that's all.'

'You need to throw off this attitude, that's what. You're grumping around like a teenager not like a mature twenty-eight year old.'

'You are, of course, entitled to your own opinion, Mother.'

'Don't take that snotty tone with me. I'm not one of your office staff.'

'Huh. That's what she said to me.'

'"She?"' Her tone was glacial and I saw exactly why the staff had held her in respect and not a little fear. She had rarely spoken to me in such a cold voice.

'I beg your pardon, Ma. I didn't mean to be rude. I meant, the countess.'

'Child,' she said, her tone back to warm. 'I can't help you if you don't tell me.' Her eyes searched my face. 'My gut tells me it's something to do with Allegra. Have you argued with her? You and she have been friends for most of her life. Try and make it up or you'll both be miserable.'

Just inside the entrance to the domestic hall a wide corridor ran the width of the complex. Open shelving and racks of pigeonholes hung on one wall, a leftover from previous times, but nevertheless useful. Two shallow but long wooden tables, one with two monitors, stood under them. A large LED panel for the domestic system occupied the wall at right angles. Five biosignatures were displayed as blips in the staff sitting room and two in the kitchen; no doubt the cook and his assistant clearing up after the evening meal I'd missed. Well, I'd grab a sandwich and a piece of honey cake. If the cook still had a moment, he might do me some pasta. I needed an early night to make up for getting in at three this morning.

I pushed open the swing door and was ready with a joke about clocking up overtime but it died on my lips. He was there all right, using a cooking slice to place three beautifully grilled *isicia omentata* on a bed of lettuce. I could smell the fish-scented *liquamen* and pine nuts the minute I stepped through the door. My stomach rumbled in in response. Westerners called them burgers, but those tasteless lumps weren't anywhere near these succulent golden ovals.

Her back to the door, a young woman was sitting on the bench at the long table. I knew those tight shoulders. Allegra's. The cook set the plate down on the table in front of her and smiled down at her as if she were a favourite daughter. As she half-turned I saw the remnant of the smile she'd sent back to him. She glanced back towards the door and flinched when she saw me. I nodded at the cook, who busied himself with his pans. After a moment's hesitation, I walked to the other side of the table and sat down opposite her.

'Eat, or they'll get cold.' I pointed at her food.

She cut them up precisely and ate methodically, but kept her eyes on her food. The cook brought us coffee and disappeared into the pantry. Allegra glanced up at me once, flushed and went back to eating. Was she still embarrassed about her punishment? She said nothing more until she'd devoured all the food on her plate. She sipped her coffee, looking at the kitchen walls, the table or nowhere in particular.

'Allegra,' I began, and stretched my hand out across the table towards her, but didn't touch her. 'I'm sorry if I upset you this morning. I wouldn't hurt you for all the world.'

'You didn't. I feel such a fool. I know you were angry on my behalf, but I didn't know how to explain it.' She took my outstretched hand and pressed it.

'You don't have to,' I said, swallowing hard.

Her eyes were full of smiles.

'You're my friend, Macrinus. I shouldn't be grouchy with you. I'm a little out of sorts at present. Maybe being at home this week will give me time to think.'

'Is anything bothering you at work?'

'Not really. Well, except Major Fausta being on my case.' She shrugged. 'Maybe she was right and I am a little arrogant.'

'Mercury crumble in ash!' I couldn't believe what she'd said. 'You are the least arrogant person I know.'

'You're biased, my friend.'

'Yes, of course I am.' I could have stayed there the rest of my life holding her hand, watching her smile at me, but we were interrupted by the cook's rumbling cough.

'I'd like to close the kitchen, *domina*, so if you wouldn't mind moving, please.'

Allegra jumped up. 'I'm so sorry, Cook. We're being thoughtless.' She grabbed her plate and cutlery and took them over to the sink.

In the corridor, she hesitated for a moment. 'Thank you, Macrinus.' She stretched up on her tiptoes, laid her hand on my shoulder and kissed my cheek. I couldn't say or do a thing. I just stared at her.

'Goodnight.' She whirled round, her hair following the sudden movement of her head like a curtain being drawn across in a hurry, and ran off.

Allegra

Bloody hell. Did Macrinus ever take that poker out of his rear? He'd just stood there like a dummy when I'd given him a peck on the cheek.

It had been the same when he'd come back from London nearly three years ago.

I'd had such a serious crush on him when I was fourteen, just before that time Dad was ill. But I'd known that somebody ten years older wouldn't look at a kid like me.

When my crazy half-sister Nicola had nearly killed my mother and aimed that gun at me up at the old castle ruins, I had one of those weird 'standing still in time' moments. I put all that kids' stuff behind me and started concentrating on what mattered – my family and my duty. My now ex-friend, Maia, laughed until she nearly crapped herself when she heard I was going into the military. She said she was too busy lunching and doing the occasional charity event to have a career. We hadn't seen each other since leaving school; I didn't miss her.

When Macrinus had been due back from his studies in London I'd checked the time of his flight and waited, half hidden in one of the huge leather chairs in the atrium. The sound of the front entrance door opening and the double bleep of the security scan were followed by a pattern of regular click-clack footsteps and case wheels squeaking. They became louder until he came out of the vestibule corridor and entered the atrium.

I jumped up to greet him, but couldn't take a single step more. The man in front of me wasn't Macrinus. He couldn't be. Tall, brown wavy hair, dark, almost black eyes; those were his. But his face was thinner, not a gram of fat. And he stood so tall and confident. Oh, gods, he was like something out of a fashion magazine. Not a sign of my friend. This stranger made me feel so disappointed; I wanted to run. But I had to say something.

'Welcome home, Macrinus,' I'd whispered. The warmth crawling up my neck into my face became unbearable. My tongue had stuck to the roof of my mouth and my brain had gone into full blank mode. He'd stared at me as if I was the dumbest creature alive. I'd closed my eyes for an instant, glanced at him and ran off.

Back in my room, I'd been so angry with myself. He would have thought I was totally dim-witted. He was my friend. How could I have been like this with him?

That was then. Now I was three years older, but he was still distant. Maybe I'd offended him somehow without realising it. It was so easy; people often took something in completely the wrong way like Major Fausta had. But Macrinus was my oldest friend. I thought I knew him and could talk to him without having to worry about what I said. Obviously not.

When I'd tried that afternoon two days ago and he'd called me '*domina*', I didn't know how I hadn't hit him. He wasn't being subservient or pseudo-subservient; he was being correct. That was how the staff was supposed to address me as the junior heir. But Macrinus? He'd put up this ten-metre wall between us and I didn't know why. And when he'd discovered me on my knees cleaning in the atrium I was so embarrassed I wanted to vanish into the ether. Stupid really. As the under-steward, he was bound to see me sometime during this week.

He'd been furious, I could see that. I know he hated not knowing everything; he always prided himself on being the most informed person in the universe. Maybe that was it or he still thought I was a little kid who needed protecting from the big bad wolves, in this case Major Fausta and Mama. I didn't blame Mama, well, not too much. I could see her logic; she'd learned the hard way and wanted me not to have such a tough path. Maybe she thought I should learn any hard lessons now rather than la*ter*. As she'd said all those years ago when I was before the court, I had to 'take it like a Mitela'. But Major Fausta was a whole other question. She had been wrong. But I'd do my best to stay off her radar in the future.

As for Macrinus, fine, if that's how he wanted it. I decided I'd be friendly but cool. But it wouldn't be easy. When he'd stretched his hand out across the kitchen table, I saw my old friend back for a few minutes, his eyes warm and comforting. But as we'd left the kitchen and I'd given him a quick peck on the cheek, he'd stared at me as if he was a tailor's dummy and didn't say a thing. Well, the hell with him.

I ignored him totally the next day, stuck my chin in the air and pretended not to see him when he walked past me in the domestic hall corridor. I had my plastic tote with dusters and cleaning products in one hand and a packet of protective gloves grasped in the other and was making my way to dusting Mama's study and its kilometres of bookshelves.

Domus Mitelarum was a mishmash of ancient and old. The last big rebuild in the late 1600s had simply surrounded what had been left of the ancient villa and the medieval extensions. It looked square and serene from the outside, but was full of corners and turns inside. Mama had her study towards the back with two original villa walls; she loved the old exposed stonework and had supervised its restoration. To get there, I had to step down a short flight of stairs, then go through an old doorway, originally one of the house side entrances. About to turn the last corner to go down the steps, I heard her say, 'Juno, Fausta, I don't know.'

I froze.

'Well, Countess, I don't know what the Hades got into her,' I heard Fausta reply. Gods, the phone was on loudspeaker – anybody could overhear. 'It's like something snapped inside her. She's so conscientious and smart normally and I couldn't believe she'd cheeked me so brazenly.'

'Like you never did me?' I heard Mama laugh.

'Yeah, but that's me.' Fausta's voice. 'Okay, I admit, she had a point, but she was beyond insubordinate in the way she put it across. I thought summary exclusion would teach her a lesson.'

'She's nineteen, she can't be good all the time. In fact, she needs to go off the rails a little.'

My mother, for Mars' sake.

'Perhaps, but she's not Miss Prissy-Arse. She joins in the mess games and drinking sessions as much as anybody.'

Gods, how embarrassing. I prayed Fausta didn't give any details. But then Mama must have done the same when she was military.

'There's one thing, though…' Fausta continued.

'What?'

'I've never seen her with anybody special. A lot of them pair up with a "special friend", but she hasn't. I wonder if she's got a sudden fit of the hormones?'

'Fausta!'

'All right, it's only an idea. No need to eat me.'

Take that, Major! I silently cheered Mama on for standing up for me.

'I'm not,' Mama said. 'But it never occurred to me. She's so focused. You sure there's nobody in the unit?'

This was unbearable. How dare they discuss my sex life, or lack of it, like a couple of old market gossips? I nearly burst through the door, but embarrassment and the training held me back.

'Okay, Fausta, thanks for the call,' came Mama's voice. 'I've put her on chores this week. Maybe that'll steady her down. Out.'

I leant back against the rough stone of the corridor and took a deep breath to calm myself. I knew Major Fausta would call, but overhearing the intimate details was something I wasn't prepared for. And they were so wrong. My hormones, as they put it, were perfectly under control. Ridiculous.

'You're very quiet, darling,' my mother said twenty minutes after I'd started removing, dusting and replacing books.

'I'm just getting on with my work.' I kept my back to her and stretched to a higher shelf. I waited for the explosion.

'Stop being a smart-ass and come and sit down.' She sighed. 'First Macro, now you. What's the air con throwing out into the house?'

I turned, put the brush down, plonked myself down on the chair on the far side of her desk and folded my hands in my lap. She gave me a long look over her reading glasses. She gestured me to come nearer, so I shuffled to the side of her desk while she shut her file and placed it on the stack of others. The spreadsheet on her browser vanished into a corner of the screen as she closed it. She pulled her glasses off and laid them on the desk.

'Okay, so tell me what's going on.'

'There's nothing to tell.'

'Really?'

'I suppose Fausta's told you what I said.'

'Major Fausta is more concerned about what's behind it. She was perfectly within her rights to exclude you. I think you got away with it lightly. In my day, it would have been a week in the cells and a disciplinary on your record.'

I rolled my eyes.

'Thin ice, Allegra,' my mother said in a neutral tone.

'Sorry,' I muttered.

'So I should damn well think so.'

She leaned forward and took my hand in both of hers. She searched my face. 'Is something more fundamental bothering you? Are you still happy at the PGSF?'

'Yes, you know I love it. It's just that sometimes I feel nobody takes any notice of anything I say or contribute.'

'That's part of being a junior lieutenant.' She laughed. 'You're the tiniest cog in the command machine – insignificant, but a vital part of keeping it going, all at the same time.'

'Huh.'

She gave my hand a little shake. 'Hey, don't worry – you'll get your promotion next year, then you'll be more comfortable. Promise.' She pinched the leg ends of the glasses together and shuffled the thin triangle back and forth across the desk surface. 'When I started, your father was commanding the anti-terrorist unit. He had nothing to do with training and didn't have a clue about the bullying and petty attacks on me. No way was I going to complain to him. But I had a record number of training injuries when I was a junior LT, some from nasty little traps set by an *optio* responsible for our military fitness and basic skills, and his ass-kissers, some from fighting back. That *optio* was Legate Vara's cousin, her "client", if you will. My comrade-in-arms Flavius had my back a lot of the time, thank Mars. In the end it got serious, so I settled it with the most terrifying link fight of my life.'

She paused and looked down.

I held my breath, not wanting to break the spell of her story.

'The optio was trying to have me thrown out or injured so I'd be medically retired. I did wonder at the time if it was Vara trying to damage your father's position. It turned out to be envy.' After a full minute's silence, she looked up. 'But that was a long time ago. Things have changed. I'm only telling you this to show that I understand about the undercurrents and petty rivalries of military life as well as the warm friendships and the comradeship of purpose. I used to pour it all out to my grandmother. She knew what it was like. I haven't told you this to bore you or belittle any of your concerns. I just want you to understand that I know where you are.'

My mother had never been hardened growing up as a Roma Novan. Despite her foster family in America being indifferent, her life had been a great deal softer there. She must have had such a difficult time when she started. I took her hand and pressed it.

'Really, there is no problem,' I reassured her. 'It's no worse than being in the last year at school. Actually, it's a great deal more fun.

Even the boys seem to have grown up.' I flashed a grin at her and received one back.

'So is there a special boy amongst them?'

Clever, Mama. Neatly done.

'No. I love most of them like brothers or cousins, but…'

'There's no spark?'

'Exactly. Sometimes, I don't think I'm cut out for, er, family life.'

Her expression tightened for an instant. You wouldn't have seen it unless you knew her well – she was that good – but I knew every pore on my mother's face. Apart from having been a very successful field officer able to hide her thoughts, she firmly believed in not commenting on other people's emotional choices. But I'd seen it – she was disappointed, no, stricken.

'Well,' she said, her features rebalanced, 'I wouldn't give up yet, darling. Nineteen's a bit young to renounce emotional pleasures. And you will be a better officer as well as a more fulfilled person.'

I felt the heat rising up my face.

'Mama, I—'

'No, listen, it's a cliché, but you haven't met the right person yet.' She made a moue. 'Trite but true.'

I swallowed hard. I loved my mother, but this was getting too personal.

'Well, Great Nonna survived without a partner for much of her life,' I said, trying to lighten the mood. 'She did all right without a grand passion.'

'Ah!'

'What?'

'That's not exactly true, Allegra. Do you remember a tall, curly-headed man who was with Senator Calavia at Great Nonna's funeral?'

'Yes, I think so. The one who threw the red rose on the pyre? He was a foreigner, Austrian like Dad's father, or something like that.'

'Hungarian. I only found out when the will was opened. She'd left a letter and a book of pressed red roses for me, one for each year since she was twenty-nine. Once she came back from a trip to Vienna distraught and locked herself in her room for the next three days. I'd always *wondered* what that had been about. I prised the rest out of Senator Calavia who'd known Great Nonna when they served together in the PGSF before and during the Great Rebellion. Let me tell you about it...'

Macrinus

The Censor's officer was not amused; he hadn't found anything apart from two overclaims for sales tax refunds – a huge sum of 268.93 solidi. In a multi-million *solidi* business, I thought that was little short of a miracle. I was sure he'd write it off and that would be that, especially with Floralia beginning tomorrow. Nobody wanted to work over such an important holiday.

Countess Carina's business manager, Paula Grania, and I exchanged a quick glance but kept passive faces. Her exec sat motionless beside her, equally neutral-faced. Galienus, technically heading our team, started to apologise, but the Censor's officer jerked his hand up which stopped Galienus in mid flow.

'I'm sorry, steward,' he snapped, 'but it's simply not good enough. If this is what we found on a cursory glimpse, I shudder to think what else there may be underlying this so-called perfect set of accounts and returns.'

He nodded towards one of his assistants.

'Dolcia Plicata will carry out an in-depth examination. Please arrange for her to have full access to corporate and personal accounts. I stress "full access".'

Galienus turned white. I thought he was going to go into cardiac arrest. 'Of course.' He paused and glanced me. His Adam's apple bounced up and down. 'Macrinus Sestinus will coordinate everything for you.'

The Censor's officer logged off his el-pad, gathered up his papers and strode out without another word, his second assistant trailing behind him. After the door closed, Galienus took a deep breath and gave Dolcia Plicata a tight smile.

'If you would wait here, I'll arrange some coffee for you. You'll excuse us for a short while.'

Petite, delicate almost, Plicata sat straight and looked completely at her ease. The only animation was the way her eyes flicked between the four of us.

'The water you have already provided will be quite sufficient, thank you.'

We filed out of the meeting room, almost holding a collective breath. On the back terrace, Grania fished in her pocket and pulled out her cigarettes. After a few puffs, she'd recovered enough to speak.

'What an arse. Just on the eve of the holiday. Everything's in perfect order. I didn't know that was a crime.' She glared at me. 'What in Hades was that tax reclaim about?'

'Nothing,' I said. 'A temp's mistake.'

'Well, you'll have to convince Miss Prissy in there that we're clean. Good luck with that.' Grania snorted, threw her cigarette to the terrace floor and stamped on it. She nodded to her exec and they left.

Galienus bent down and picked up the crushed stub from the otherwise immaculate terrace.

'You'd better get on with it,' he said. 'I'll tell the countess.'

Dolcia Plicata was as precise as she looked. She requested to be left alone to compile her enquiry plan and asked me to attend in exactly two hours' time. I dithered around the office, reviewing the farm estate returns for the past quarter and the projected budget for the business travel for the next. Fifteen minutes before the appointed time, I finished my fortifying cup of coffee, gathered up my summary files and el-pad, locked my office door and made my way back to the meeting room ready to fend off what she had prepared.

'Please, Macrinus Sestinus, come in.' She extended her arm, inviting me to take the seat opposite her as if I was the visitor and this was her office. Her dark neat head bent over two sheets of typescript that must have been printed on the slim barrel-shaped portable printer set at exact right angles to her laptop. She signed the second sheet, stapled them with the tiniest stapler I'd ever seen and handed them to me.

'Here are my initial questions. Please gather the information together for me for my return at ten a.m. tomorrow morning.'

I scanned the pages. It was mid-afternoon now. We would need to work all night. I glanced at her and saw she was watching me intently – for my reaction, I supposed. Her dark eyes gleamed, as if assessing her prey. That was ridiculous and a cliché, but all the same, I instinctively felt we'd have to be very careful with this one.

The two clerks who had volunteered and I were just starting the second page. I glanced at the clock; it was nine p.m. We were doing well, so I told them to break for twenty minutes. I called the kitchen and asked for more coffee and sandwiches. The cook had put one of his staff on to provide us with food whenever we needed. Countess Carina had not been at all happy according to Galienus. She'd described the Censor's office in very colourful terms and ordered all possible support from everybody on this. I think sometimes she thought she was still in the PGSF combating threats and attacks. Well, she wasn't far wrong in this instance. I stood up and stretched my neck and shoulders. Gods, I could do with a drink, but I'd have to manage with the inevitable water and keep a clear head.

At the knock on the door, the younger clerk went and opened it. To my utter surprise, Allegra walked in. She carried a large tray heaped with ham salad baguette sandwiches, cups of steaming soup and a large jug of lemonade with spices and honey. The two clerks gawped.

'Cook says you must eat everything or he'll be offended,' she said. Her face was a little pinker than usual, but perfectly composed. She set the tray down in the space the older clerk scrambled to make for her. As I reached for a sandwich, I inadvertently touched her hand stretching out for my glass. She stopped, jug poised in mid-air. After the tiniest hesitation, she carried on pouring the drink. As she handed me the full glass, she brought her eyes up to meet mine. They shone copper brown, the green almost drowned out. The gold flecks danced inside the brown, drawing me in. I took the glass from her trembling hand, put it down on the desk and reclaimed her hand. I raised it to my lips and kissed it softly.

She sighed, almost in release. I wanted to do nothing more than bring my other hand up and reach for her waist. She gazed steadily at me and her lips parted slightly as she whispered, 'Oh.'

A loud rasp, a cry. The sound of a hand slapping a desk. I wrenched myself away from Allegra's gaze to frown at the interruption. The younger clerk, Lucia, was choking; her hands were fluttering round her neck. Allegra snapped her head round and snatched her hand away from mine. She grabbed the clerk's shoulder, spun her round and delivered five sharp blows with the heel of her hand between her shoulder blades. The young clerk spluttered for a second, and pellets of bread and greens dribbled out of her mouth. She gave a deep cough and the rest followed. I grabbed some tissues and passed them to Allegra. She wiped the clerk's face but the girl couldn't stop crying. She grasped Allegra's hand, looking into her face and burst into fresh sobbing.

After several minutes, I said, 'For Mars' sake, Lucia, get a grip.'

Allegra shot me a death look. She put her arm round the girl's shoulders and sat her down in my chair. She rubbed her back, and murmured reassuring words. The girl sipped the water Allegra handed her. The older clerk stared. I flicked my fingers at him to get back to work and he scuttled back to his desk.

'You saved my life, *domina*,' the girl said after a minute and gazed at Allegra with an adoring look usually saved by the pious for the gods.

'No, no,' Allegra said. 'It was just some food that went down the wrong way. Now take some shallow breaths and some sips of water. But slowly.' Allegra looked at me. 'This poor girl's had a frightening experience. You'll have to let her go and rest.'

'She'll be fine now. Don't worry.' I turned to the clerk. 'How do you feel now, Lucia?'

'Much better, sir, thank you. I must get back to my spreadsheet.'

I gave her a sardonic look. She was more devoted to her triple overtime pay, I reckoned, than any columns of figures.

'Such devotion, Lucia,' I replied.

She had the grace to blush.

I turned to Allegra. 'If you will excuse us, we'll carry on.'

'You are joking,' she shot at me. 'You think she'll be able to concentrate on columns of figures after nearly choking to death?'

'It wasn't that bad, and she didn't.'

'Gods, you're all heart, aren't you?'

'I'm just not making an uncomfortable incident into a major casualty case.'

'Well, I want her to rest.'

'She's needed here. She's agreed she's fit to work on and that's final.'

'Oh, really? Suppose I make that a formal order?'

'Don't go there, Allegra.'

'You will release her on medical grounds, and immediately.'

I could have shaken her.

'Due to the urgent circumstances, I must decline, *domina*.' I put every gram of sarcasm I could find into my reply.

Her face muscles tensed and pink blotches appeared on her cheeks. She sent me a look that could have lit a funeral pyre by itself, spun round and slammed the door as she left. As soon as we'd finished with the Censor's investigation, I knew I'd be packing my bags. Maybe even sooner.

Dolcia Plicata looked serene as she glided across the atrium. Yesterday's sharp suit had been replaced by a casual jacket and skirt, and she wore her hair down. For a tax inspector she looked a lot less threatening than before.

'You must have been burning the midnight oil to prepare so much,' she said and gave me a proper smile.

'It's a team effort,' I replied. 'And I'm very lucky in mine. Unfortunately, one of my assistants was taken ill but the other clerk and I completed your questions by midnight. So not too, er, taxing.'

She laughed at my stupid joke and the atmosphere became more relaxed, which was of course the whole idea. She set her laptop and files out as precisely as the day before, but I noticed she wore bright red nail polish and several rings on her slim fingers, but no companion's band.

We worked for a couple of hours, then broke for a sandwich lunch. I was feeling reasonably optimistic about how the meeting was going as I piled the plates back on the tray, when a message flashed up on my laptop screen: Countess Carina asking me to attend for a short meeting at my earliest convenience. Hades. I just hoped she would give me a reference after firing me.

'Would you excuse me for half an hour?'

'Yes, of course.' Plicata smiled at me. 'In fact, I need to write up a summary of my notes, so perhaps we could say an hour from now?'

Countess Carina received me in her private sitting room.

'Thank you for coming in the middle of what must be a trying day, but I wanted to speak with you as soon as possible. How is it going with the Censor's inspector? Grim, I would think.'

'No, *domina*, surprisingly not so far. I know it's probably part of their technique, but she's very friendly, although, of course, completely professional.'

'You be careful, Macro. Your mother was smart with these people, but she was a nervous wreck last time by the time they'd finished.'

'Everything's up to date and properly filed,' I said. 'I really can't see why we're being investigated. Maybe that's it – we look too perfect.'

'Hm. Well, you tell me immediately if you need any support of any kind, including a lawyer.'

She looked down into the fire grate and fiddled with her signet ring. It was heavy gold with an entwined myrtle leaf pattern; legend had it the original Mitelus had worn it when he'd led the first settlers from ancient Rome all those centuries ago. Whatever the truth of it, his descendant's hand and fingers were strong enough to wear it. I waited.

'I'm pleased it's going as well as it could, but I didn't call you here to discuss that. Sit down, Macro, no sorry, Macrinus. I've asked you here to make you a formal apology.' She sighed. 'Allegra was wrong to give you that order last night, and you were completely right to refuse it.'

'Stunned' wasn't anywhere near accurate to describe how I felt.

'How—'

'She came running to me full of indignation, but I told her exactly where to get off. It was entirely your judgement call.'

'She was naturally concerned for the girl and I admire her for that.'

'It was an abuse of power, a small one, granted, and made from her heart. She was overwrought for some reason and I think it made her act thoughtlessly.'

'The clerk was upset, *domina*, so I sent her to bed anyway. She's fine this morning, even a little pert, but she calmed down when I gave her a stack of files to work on.'

'Well, you have my thanks for acting resolutely. I don't know what Allegra's problem is at the moment.' She looked across at me. 'You've been close to her all her life. Any ideas?'

I didn't know what to say. I couldn't analyse my own feelings about Allegra, let alone discuss her emotional state with her mother who was looking at me expectantly. The two of them had always been so close. You could see it in the warmth of their smiles to each other, their mutual physical ease, the almost unconscious fitting round each other as they talked and moved.

If I said nothing, she'd think I was stupid or hiding something. If I said something bland and crass, I'd look uncaring. Damn Allegra for putting me in this position.

'I can't offer you any insight, *domina*, I'm sorry. She seems a little agitated. Perhaps she's upset at her exclusion. My impression is that she thought it unfair.' I tried very hard to keep my voice neutral.

'And you don't?'

Jupiter, she was sharp.

'It's not for me to say. I have no experience of the military, but it seemed peremptory.'

'Major Fausta is fairly relaxed and invites contributions, so I figure Allegra must have really stepped over the mark. Everybody does it at some time, sure, but I sense something a lot deeper. She's so jumpy. I wonder if something of the Nicola business is surfacing at last. Maybe she should have counselling.'

'Allegra is one of the most focused, thoughtful people I know. No way is she a head case.'

'My, my, you're quick to defend her. But you always were her champion.'

'I apologise, *domina*, I didn't mean to be rude,' I said. Hades. I felt warm and uncomfortable under her gaze. 'Perhaps she's had an argument with a colleague or a lovers' tiff.'

Jupiter's balls, why had I said that? How bloody stupid could I be? She gave me a sharp look and frowned, but didn't say anything for a few moments.

'Very well, Macrinus. I think I understand. Don't let me delay you any longer.' She got to her feet and held her hand out to me. I jumped up, shook the outstretched hand and left. And cursed myself all the way back to my office.

Allegra

When I'd run to Mama to report Macrinus's unfair treatment of his clerk, she'd listened without interrupting. She'd looked down at the newspaper she'd been reading but said nothing for a good minute. She looked up and fixed her gaze on my face.

'You acted so quickly in saving the clerk from choking. Most people would have frozen. That was very well done.'

'It was just the training.'

'No, it was the instinct of your kind heart.' She paused. 'I've always been so proud of you, your achievements and how you've dealt with all the crap that's been thrown at you.'

I could hear a 'but' coming.

'I never thought I would need to say this to you, Allegra. Ever.' She looked up. 'I'm not going to say I'm disappointed. That's such a feeble word. No, I'm angry. I'll put it down to your current weird mood, but I'm so mad I could kick you all the way back to the barracks myself. Not that you deserve the privilege of serving in the PGSF any more.'

'Mama—'

'Be quiet.'

My mother looked at me in the way Great Nonna Aurelia had reserved for when she'd suspended one of the Mitela cousins from family protection and events for a year – the ultimate condemnation.

'Do you have any idea what I'm talking about?'

I shook my head. She raised an eyebrow. I nodded slowly.

'And?'

I swallowed hard. 'I shouldn't have given Macrinus that order,' I muttered.

'That's a third of the way. Keep going.'

What else was there?

'Why was it wrong?' she said.

'Well,' I squirmed, 'it wasn't my call, I suppose, but—'

'Because?'

'It's his office and his staff.'

'How would you like it if Major Fausta ordered a member of your Active Response Team to do something or stop doing something in front of you and the other enlisted troops?'

'She's perfectly within her rights to do that,' I shot back, seeing a way out.

'No doubt, but Fausta wouldn't do anything so discourteous or ham-fisted, not unless it was extremely urgent or in the middle of an operational crisis. She would instruct you to do it. Well, the chain of command exists in every organisation, including here.'

She was right, of course, and I hated that fact.

'You undermined his authority in front of his staff. For that, you will apologise to Macrinus in front of all of his clerks.'

Juno, the humiliation, but I knew in my heart she was right. Tears in my eyes, but mortified in case they escaped, I turned to go.

'Stay where you are. We're not done. I love you so much, Allegra. I'm your mother, but I'm also the head of our family. I can't hold it all together if everybody doesn't play their part. You have a particular responsibility as my direct heir to set a good example. In case you haven't worked it out yet, I have to reprimand you for an abuse of power. Yes, legally, as my heir you have the right to issue an instruction or order to any of our employees or family members, but every time you do, you have to think carefully about whether it's a reasonable, practical or balanced one.

'As foreign-raised, I had to learn it the awkward way. Luckily, I had Great Nonna to keep me straight. You've been bred as a Roman and I thought you'd got it. You seemed to do it naturally. This business with Macrinus makes me doubt it now. Please do not give any instructions to the household aside from the minimalist day-to-day ones. If you need to diverge from that, you come to me first. Understood?'

As I walked back I couldn't believe how hard Mama had been. I'd seen that incinerating look once before when she'd faced off my mad half-sister Nicola several years ago up at the castle ruins. I'd prayed I would never see that aimed at me. Well, now I had and I felt barbecued.

I knew I'd been wrong the second after I'd spoken to Macrinus. What in Hades I thought I was doing, I didn't know. I'd felt an irresistible and frightening urge to push it, just to see how far he would take it. But I'd gone so far past too far that I just wanted to walk off the edge of the cliff and it would all be over.

When he'd taken my hand and kissed it moments before his clerk started choking, I'd felt a soft tingle run up my arm. His dark eyes shone black and I thought I recognised something that I couldn't put a name to. A kind of coming home or settling. We'd been friends for years, but this was different. I'd held my breath to see what would happen next but all I could see was the smile in his eyes and on his lips and feel the warmth of his hand. I had no idea whether I stood there for a few seconds or a few hours.

Then the clerk had started choking and everything broke apart.

After a restless night's sleep, I went to Macrinus's office next morning, but after I'd asked to see him, the three clerks exchanged a glance. After a few moments, the senior one said Macrinus would be tied up in a meeting all day but he'd leave a message for him. Maybe I was being sensitive, but I thought I saw a speculative smile on Lucia's face. I was about to say something, then I remembered Mama's instructions. I swallowed, thanked the senior clerk and left.

I trudged back to the kitchen, picked up my plastic holdall and went into the atrium to start on the endless plate glass window panels. As I polished, I began to rub furiously. I'd hyped myself up to apologise to Macrinus, then he wasn't there. Now I'd have to wait until he'd finished his damned meeting.

I came back after munching a quick sandwich and carried on with the other windows. The atrium was in the eighteenth-century rebuild part of the house and had floor-to-ceiling windows either side of the sliding panels. Luckily, I only had to do the lower halves; one of the permanent staff would get the portable scaffold out tomorrow and clean the top halves. Gods, it would take hours. I was towards the far end, half behind the curtains, when I heard two sets of footsteps: one firm, wide stride, so male, the other a shorter stride, a louder click-clack of heeled shoes, so female. I turned round slowly, careful not to let the curtains move.

Macrinus and the tax office woman, Plicata. She was tiny, her features doll-like. She was like one of those impossibly slender idealised bronze statues in Great Nonna's display cabinet. As he bent over to shake her hand, she smiled up at him, a warm, attractive, inviting smile. He smiled back, tilted his head as he listened to what she said next. He took out his phone and tapped something in. She laid her hand on his forearm. How dare she touch him so intimately? He smiled on like an idiot, fascinated by her.

She gave a little wave, walked off and he watched her cross to the vestibule. I'd been gripping the plastic spray bottle so tightly it buckled and slipped from my hand, landing on the marble floor with a thunk.

Juno! What was the matter with me? A rookie mistake from lack of control.

'Allegra?' He turned.

'Er, hi.' I looked over his shoulder. I was too embarrassed to look him in the eye. 'Have you finished your meeting? I need to have a few minutes of your time.'

'Of course. What is it?'

'Can we go to your office?'

He gestured for me to precede him. As we walked across the atrium, my courage nearly failed me. I stopped and he didn't. He caught me in his arms.

'Sorry,' I mumbled, pulling away from him.

'Are you okay?'

I nodded. How easy it was to lie.

In the general office, he crossed over to his own door at the side and opened it to usher me in, but I stopped where I was.

'I have something to say which concerns you all.'

The three clerks swivelled round in their chairs to face me. Macrinus's face was impassive, but his eyes tightened slightly.

'I— I would like to make a formal apology to Macrinus Sestinus for my rudeness last night.' I looked at Lucia. 'I hope you are now fully recovered.'

Macrinus took a step forward, but I couldn't bear it if he were to say something conciliatory, so I turned and fled.

At seven the following morning, I was back at the breakfast table in the dining room in my light fatigues ready to go back to my normal life. I would leave all this embarrassment and stupidity behind, thank the gods. According to the calendar on my phone the rest of the week was mostly tactical training, part classroom, part fieldwork. I'd written my teaching *notes* the week before and I'd received a merit in that subject at the Land Forces Officers' Training School, so I hoped I'd be able to slot in the schedule without too much hassle.

I'd also been rostered to lead a couple of evening urban patrols in support of the *custodes*. It was Floralia, when people became extra drunk and extra stupid. It wasn't the *custodes*' fault they couldn't manage – they couldn't be everywhere this week with all the street theatricals and the parades going on. No, the ungodly would be out in their droves. But we'd be there with our slightly more robust touch. I smiled. Few tangled with Praetorians. As long as nobody threw up on us, it should be fairly routine.

I leaned back and stretched my arms upwards. That run this morning to the end of the parkland behind the garden had been liberating after a week of indoor drudgery.

I started when my hand was caught and whirled round to see my mother's smiling face. In a strange way I was disappointed. How could that be? She might be firm when she had to be, but she was my lodestar, my champion, my home.

'Ready to go back?' she said.

'Yes, thank Mars.'

'Ha! Well, I hope you don't feel too down about this week.' She pressed my hand as I brought it down. 'Major Fausta will be pleased to see you, I think.'

'To be honest, Mama, it's not been the best week of my life, but you were right. I've been an idiot.'

She gave my hand a little shake and bent and kissed my forehead.

'Go carefully,' she said.

Macrinus

She's gone. I didn't know whether to be pleased, relieved or desolate. I wouldn't see her for at least a month unless something extraordinary happened.

Once the tax investigation was finished and we'd received the formal discharge letter almost immediately from the Censor's office, I saw Dolcia Plicata for a date. She was sharp, fun and smart and we shared a lot professionally. After a meal at the Onyx, we went on to Goldlights, a club where the music was so loud it sucked the air out of your ears, but the band rocked, almost literally. Dolcia laughed, her eyes sparkled at the comedian in between acts. We danced, her skin warm under my hand on her bare back. She looked up into my face with such an alluring smile it almost took my breath away. Mercury, she was an enticing woman. I drew her closer, so her sleek black head rested on my neck, my lips on her hair.

After the dance, we settled back at the table with fresh drinks. She laid her hand over mine. Her lips were slightly parted, her eyes inviting.

'My place is near here,' she said softly. 'Or am I going too fast for a first date?'

I took her hand and kissed the fingertips.

'Not at all,' I replied. I stood and held out my hand and she set hers in mine.

She was right, her address was only four hundred metres away. It was a twentieth-century building, built after the Great War that ended in 1935. Plain, regular, but with little balconies decorated with plants trailing down. Now, subdued yellow light shone from lantern-shaped lamps fixed along the front at first-floor level.

At the building door, she turned to me. Before she could say anything, I circled her waist, pulled her to me and kissed her.

'Gods, Macrinus, where did you learn to kiss like that?' She grinned.

'Misspent student life in London.' I smiled back.

She laughed and turned to tap her building code into the retro keypad but paused. Footsteps – boots – several of them. Custodes on their standard Saturday night patrol. When I'd been in London, the police had always gathered a good crop of drunks on Saturdays. I glanced sideways.

Hades.

It was boots all right, but not the *custodes*. Five figures, men, no, two were women, all masked for party-going. Only party-goers didn't run towards you brandishing heavy duty rubber torches.

'Quick, get inside,' I hissed at Dolcia. 'I'll buy us a few seconds.'

'Gods, Macrinus, don't you think I'm trying.' Her voice was shrill as she jabbed at the old-fashioned keypad. She fluffed it.

'Want some help, darlin'?' one of the men shouted. 'We're good at getting into tight entrances.' The others joined in his dirty laugh, then formed a ring round us. I turned to face them, keeping Dolcia behind me. Body odour several days old hit us. Their eyes gleamed. Greedy eyes, searching us.

'Keep away from us – we have no money,' I shouted.

'Yeah? And I'm Mercury's fuck-buddy!' the nearest man said and sneered.

One of the women shot her hand out and tugged the diamond stud from Dolcia's ear. Dolcia screamed like a Fury. Blood dribbled from her earlobe.

I swung my fist at the nearest figure. The next second, pain exploded in my middle and I collapsed on the ground. Hard. Kicks to my ribs. Ah, my chest shrieked with pain. I could hardly gasp for breath. Dolcia screamed again. Hands rifled my pockets and heaved my shoes off. I tried to roll away, but one of them thumped the side of my head. I brought my arms up to defend myself. My head was swimming. Passing out...

Jupiter save us. If only he could.

Suddenly, the kicking stopped. Running boots. Sharp commands. A shot. Thumps, bodies hitting the ground, obscenities. Dolcia shrieking, 'Five of them – one went that way.'

I took a deep breath. Mistake. Pain seared through me like a hot knife.

'Easy now.' A man's voice. 'Medic,' he shouted out to the side of me. A younger man bent over me and touched my head and my neck, then started dabbing with a cold cloth. Another figure dropped to its knees beside me. Her hand. I knew her hand instantly.

'It's okay, Macrinus. You're safe,' Allegra said.

Praetorians. Thank the gods.

Despite the kicking, none of my ribs was broken and I was able to sit, then stand up. I didn't want to go to hospital, just somewhere quiet. Dolcia hugged the wall and kept glancing at the Praetorians. She shrank back even though one of the female guards was gently urging her to drink some water. I wasn't worried about them myself – I'd grown up with them all around me. Many Roma Novans had some kind of connection with one of the military or police services, even though compulsory national service had long been abandoned, but not so close up.

I watched as Allegra slotted her nightstick back in the leather lo*op* on her belt next to her pistol holster. Four figures in camouflage fatigues were quietly talking; one was tapping into a small el-pad. Another one had recovered my leather shoes and I slipped my feet back in, almost losing my balance. The guard next to Allegra shot his arm out to steady me.

Her face now wore a neutral expression when she turned to me, her arms crossed and legs braced.

'Well, Macrinus Sestinus,' she said in a clipped tone, ignoring Dolcia. 'This was unfortunate. Why were you on the open street at this hour? Don't you know it's safer to get a cab?'

'It wasn't worth it from the club to my friend's place. And it's a warm night.'

'This is the last night of Floralia. And you're ambling along in expensive clothes and she's decked out like a jewellery advert. Surely nobody is that stupid – or were you just too busy to notice?' She smirked, looking from me to Dolcia and back again.

Dolcia glanced at me, then at the four Praetorians. I wouldn't have said she was panicking, but she looked nervous. Much as I wanted to, I wasn't going to have a shouting match with Allegra in the middle of the street. It would just upset Dolcia.

Allegra jerked her head in Dolcia's direction. 'Is she now capable of entering her code? Or has she completely lost it? Perhaps she's only a counting machine unable to function in the real world.' She raised one eyebrow and looked down her long Mitela nose at Dolcia nervously jabbing at the keypad.

'I— Oh, thank Mercury,' Dolcia blurted out as the door clicked. She pushed it hard and almost fell into the lobby.

I turned round to Allegra. My fists balled by themselves.

'Obviously, we're very grateful to you for helping us, but was that really necessary?' I thrust my face into hers.

The *optio* stepped towards me, but Allegra held up her hand. She almost looked smug. 'We always try to give irresponsible citizens safety advice, even though they might not welcome it. A pity, but you just can't help some people.' She jerked her head in Dolcia's direction. 'You better run along now, Macrinus. She looks a little anxious. Goodnight.'

'Who the hell was that?' Dolcia almost shouted at me as we waited for the lift.

'Calm down, just an officious Praetorian. Forget her. We have much more important things *to* do.' Despite the throbbing headache, I put my arm round Dolcia's waist. She was trembling, but shrugged my arm off.

'She knew you.' Dolcia's eyes, smudged with ruined make-up and dried tears, searched my face.

'Well, my mother and employer are both ex-PGSF so inevitably I know some of them. Look, don't worry. It's just a bad coincidence. Come on, we could both do with a brandy.'

'And I think you knew her.'

I hesitated. For some reason, I didn't want to admit it.

'Let's forget her,' I said and smiled down at her. 'What have you got to drink upstairs?'

'You know what, Macrinus? Forget tonight. You can find your own way out.'

I don't know how I reached home without exploding. The taxi came quickly, but the whole twenty minutes' ride was taken up with variations on the image of me throttling Allegra. I pitched up at the service door of Domus Mitelarum, glared into the optical reader and slapped my hand onto the palm reader. Inevitably it rejected me. I calmed down and laid it on a second time. The sensor beeped and I was in.

In my flat, I peeled off my muddy and torn evening suit and limped into the shower. Pluto, apart from the cut on my face, my body was covered in red and purple patches; some were already turning black.

Bypassing the analgesics, I threw a double whisky down my throat. Dolcia was the first time I'd come near to forgetting Allegra. Well, not forgetting her entirely, but possibly finding somebody more compatible, more accessible. Although Allegra's troops had saved us getting imperially beaten up, she'd screwed up any chance for me with Dolcia.

To Hades with her.

I'd send Dolcia the best bouquet I could find tomorrow and invite her out to dinner after Floralia somewhere out of town where we wouldn't be interrupted by riff-raff or snotty Praetorians. Whether she'd accept or not was another question.

Next morning, fuelled by several cups of strong coffee with painkillers on the side, I was hobbling across the atrium on the way to the office when I heard the front door close. Footsteps from a firm stride echoed on the marble floor in the vestibule and the tall figure of Conradus Mitelus carrying a briefcase entered the atrium.

Allegra's father.

He looked tired – from the flight, I supposed. He was only in his early fifties, but his hair was almost white, a few blond streaks here and there.

'Salve, young Macro. You're up early.'

His hazel eyes were so like Allegra's my heart twinged. Now those eyes studied my face.

'You look a bit rough. Late night?'

He might not still be the Praetorian Guard Special Forces legate, but he could sniff out a ripple from a hundred metres.

'Not really, sir, just collecting my thoughts. We've had a trying time with the Censor's office over the past week or so although that's settled now, I hope. Also, some street thugs tried to rob me and my date last night, but it's only a few bruises.'

'Mars' balls! Did you report the attack?'

'No, a Praetorian patrol intervened.'

'Oh, well done them.'

If only he knew how his precious daughter had behaved. No way was I going to tell him.

He looked at me steadily.

'Anything else?'

I shook my head.

'Very well,' he said. 'Carry on then.' As I went to pass him, he caught my arm. 'If you ever want an off-the-record talk to another man, you know you can come to me at any time.'

'Thank you, sir, but everything is fine.'

Fine. Everything is fine. That's what *she* always said, just like her mother, when everything had fallen down the deep pit of Tartarus. And they used the English word which made the point twice.

Back in the office, I emailed the clerks their tasks. A full inventory and stocktake for a start. The senior clerk could produce a half-yearly projection for the businesses, including the farm and international interests, and I'd schedule a meeting with Grania, the Mitela business manager, within the next week to set the next year's strategy.

Apart from the bruises and muscle ache, I wouldn't have time to go out and have late nights.

Allegra

'Pluto, Allegra, snap out of it.'

Diana Sergilia was my comrade, my oppo, my friend, but she was behaving like an arse-ache at the moment. I thought we were enjoying a quiet beer in the mess. It was half empty and I wanted some support, not a head-bashing.

'Sleep with him or ditch him, but just give the rest of us a break.' She looked at me with her dark eyes and tight mouth. 'If you start going weird again, Fausta'll have you out permanently. Then you'll have to work for a living.' Her faced cleared and she chuckled. 'In your case, having to traipse round being a good little junior countess with your mother, being nice to people all the time. Think of the strain of that.'

I batted her lightly with my arm.

'When I saw him being attacked, I just ran forward on instinct. We had four of the bastards all down and cuffed in under a minute. The fifth managed to get twenty metres before we got her. I let the *optio* read them their rights – I was too angry. The medic said Macrinus had nothing broken, thank the gods. Then I saw he was with that horrible tax woman,' I said. 'I felt as if she was poaching on my territory. I wanted to kick her arse all the way back to the Censor's office.'

'Wasn't he grateful for your intervention?'

'Yes, but I just couldn't stop myself being rude to him and that woman and it all came out wrong. Talk about cock-up!'

'I understand, Legra, but gods, you're behaving like a bloody teenager. You've got it really bad.'

Yes, I had, and I'd had it bad all my life.

Now that Floralia was over, Major Fausta piled on the battle tactics exercise.

'There is no such thing as can't – only won't, or insufficiently trained and equipped,' she'd said when she gave the forty of us the exercise briefing. 'The last two, we're taking care of, but the "won't" or rather the "will" is up to you. Just let me know if that's a problem and I'll find you a nice little dishwashing job somewhere.'

There were a few murmurings, one chuckle. She rostered Sergilia and me to lead opposing teams. Mama said Fausta was the cleverest woman she knew. All I knew was how hard she drove us. And in the middle of it all, just as my team had fended off a hard attack, with ordnance flashing and exploding around us, she set us a fiendish manual coding task and kept changing the signals frequencies.

On the afternoon of the third day, Sergilia's troops were pursuing mine back to our defensive fallback area after we'd snatched their marker. Just as we were weaving in and out of the trees, a rabbit ran out of a burrow in front of me and I tripped over the bloody thing. I smacked down on the ground. Pain jabbed through my ankle. I gasped with the sharpness of it. Boots were pounding in my direction so I scrambled up and tried to run.

'Arm round my shoulder, ma'am,' my centurion barked. 'We need to move.'

'Yes,' I gasped. Then I nearly screamed. 'No, go on without me. No way can you get back to the safe area with me.'

'Grab hold of your weapon and count to ten,' he said. I started, then found myself flying through the air and landing bent over his shoulder. He started running. After fifty metres, I could hear him grunting with the effort, but in a hundred, we were back in our safe area, thank the gods.

'Let's look at that ankle.' The medic bustled around and went to unfasten my boot.

I glared at him.

'If that boot comes off, I'll never get it on again,' I said. But I could feel my flesh pressing against the leather on all sides.

'If we don't get that boot off now, we'll have to cut it off.'

Merda.

The cold gel pack numbed most of the pain as I bounced along in the short wheelbase on the way back to the city, but did nothing for my resentment. Apart from that last section attack, I was pretty sure my troop was beating Sergilia's. Well, my centurion would take over. Pelo was in his forties, but he was extremely fit. Apparently, he'd served with my mother as a young soldier when they went on exercise to the UK. That was another problem. Everybody expected me to live up to her.

'Bed rest, young lady,' the doctor said, back in the unit sick bay. 'No break according to the X-ray, but a nasty wrench. The technician will be in to do the first session of electrotherapy in about an hour.'

She switched off the main light and left a night light to cast a dull yellow glow in the corner. Pluto in Tartarus. Once out of this bed and strapped up, I'd be stuck to a desk for weeks. Better than being sent home, I supposed. I couldn't bear to face Macrinus after I'd been such an arse to him in that street patrol.

What in Hades was he doing out with that tax woman? She was pretty enough but looked as if she wanted to get her claws into him and keep them hooked there. He could do so much better than that. Well, if that's the sort he liked, then that was that. I sniffed.

'What are you doing here, Dad?'

My father, Conradus Mitelus, former Praetorian legate, could walk into this building whenever he liked. Technically, he was a civilian, but I'd like to have seen somebody try to stop him. He bent down and kissed my cheek before pulling up the moulded plastic chair to the side of the bed.

'Come to see you, silly.' He grinned at me. 'You know it's going to take some time to live down tripping over a rabbit, don't you?'

The warmth spread up my neck.

'I've already had Major Fausta in here humming Run, rabbit, run,' I grumped.

He burst out laughing, then stroked my cheek with the back of his fingers.

'Well, you won't have to put up with that for a bit. You're coming home for a few days where you can be spoiled rotten. You'll also be out of the medics' hair.'

'No!'

'What? Why on earth not?' He studied my face a little too intently. 'You haven't fallen out with your mother, have you?'

'No, of course not.'

'Well?'

'I'm fine here. Honestly.'

'"Fine"? That's what your mother says when everything's gone to Hades. As do you.' He scrutinised my face for a few moments. 'Now tell me the truth. And no bullshit.'

'I—'

'Yes?' Now he was frowning at me. The skin on his face tightened, pushing his cheekbones out to make his face look as fierce as an eagle.

I looked down and picked at the bed sheet.

'I argued with Macrinus and was snotty with him when I was out on night patrol in the city when he was being mugged,' I said in one quick burst.

'That was you, was it? Strange, he didn't mention it when I asked him about the attack. What on earth did you say to him?'

'I don't know what came over me.' I felt the tears run down my face. 'I was so horrible.' Dad stood, leant over the bed and folded me into his arms. I sobbed my heart out against his chest as I had done as a little girl.

Half an hour later, I was wheeled down to the garages in an old metal-tubing hospital wheelchair and into Dad's four-by-four. As the main gates opened at Domus Mitelarum twenty minutes after that, I was horrified to see Macrinus standing in the courtyard with his mother's chair – an electronic wonder machine.

'Gods, no,' I muttered.

'Get a grip, love,' Dad said as he drew up by the garages. 'Nobody died of embarrassment.'

'You don't understand.'

'You're wrong. I do.' He took my hand in his. 'I nearly lost your mother because of that kind of stupidity. Twice. Once, I couldn't face telling her about Aunt Silvia and the children—'

'Why was that a problem?'

'I thought that as she was brought up in the EUS as an American she wouldn't understand the Roma Novan family system and would be repelled by it.'

'Why?'

'Think about it. Their different marriage and relationship customs, their strong patriarchal slant.'

'Weird.'

'Yes, but that's how they are. The second time, I just couldn't believe she'd been able to carry out the dangerous undercover operation she did. I didn't have faith in her. To my great luck, she rescued me from my stupidity.' He stared out of the window, his eyes unfocused as he was seeing something in the far distance. 'And has kept doing it for the past twenty-odd years.' After a moment, he turned round to me. 'Come on, showtime, as she says.' My father's eyes gleamed and he gave a wicked little smile. 'We can't keep poor

Macrinus waiting or he'll think you don't want to speak to him. You won't get what your heart desires – whatever that is – unless you get out there and seize it with both hands.'

Macrinus

As her father eased her into Ma's chair, her face flushed red. Was it the medication or something else? But she wouldn't meet my eyes. I navigated the chair carefully through the rooms using the hydra suspension on max, but she let out a little yelp as we passed over a low stone threshold on the way to the lift. My heart clenched. I would gladly have taken the pain for her.

Up in her room, her mother was waiting, a welcoming smile playing on her lips. I parked the chair and watched her parents lift her out. As I left the room, Conradus Mitelus gave me a warm smile.

'Come up and see her later, Macrinus,' he said. 'Knowing Allegra, she'll be bored out of her mind within a couple of hours and will be pleased to chat to an old friend. Besides, I think she has something to say to you.' He gave his daughter a stern look. She bowed her head, her soft hair falling to hide the expression on her face. The countess drew her eyebrows together and glanced at her husband with a question in her eyes. He shook his head. I was out of the door and in the lift on the landing before either of them could say another word.

Studying the half-yearly projection the senior clerk had produced seemed to be incredibly tedious that morning. I fortified myself twice with coffee but seemed to have lost all enthusiasm for something I usually enjoyed. I decided to take an early lunch. Giving myself the excuse of stretching my legs, I went to the kitchen to order it myself.

Hades. My mother was sitting at the long table chatting to the cook. But I couldn't escape.

'Macrinus!' She glanced at her watch. 'Is everything all right?'

She looked at me as if she was reading into my innermost thoughts.

'Perfectly, Ma,' I replied as smoothly as I could. 'I just wanted to get out of my chair for a few minutes.' I turned to the cook. 'Could I have an early lunch? Just some soup or fish and olive bread.' I gave him my best smile.

'Early meeting this afternoon?' Ma said.

'No, I just felt hungry.'

'Why didn't you send one of the juniors to fetch you something?'

'They were all busy with the tasks I set them.'

'I see.'

She shot me a strange look. Damn.

The cook tipped a portion of chicken smelling of tarragon and a hint of garlic out of the pan onto a plate already half full of salad – fresh mint, coriander, parsley with greens and walnuts. Allegra's favourite. He placed it on a set tray.

'I'll just get Countess Allegra's lunch out of the way then I'll sort yours out. Don't worry, I'll send it over to the office.' He raised his hand to call one of the house stewards. I leapt up.

'I'll take it up to her. Leave mine for now.'

His mouth didn't quite fall open, but I grabbed the tray before he could let even a word escape. The last thing I heard as I left the kitchen was my mother calling my name.

I knocked on Allegra's door, but she didn't answer. And again, but heard nothing. Well, I couldn't stand around in the corridor like some teenager, so I eased the door handle down with my elbow. Inside, the apricot curtains were blowing gently in the breeze. Allegra was in her bed, one shoulder uncovered by the pastel duvet, the other arm crooked, supporting her head. Her short lashes rested on her cheeks either side of her nose still freckled from childhood. She looked about fifteen. I put the tray down on the side table and crept towards the door.

'Don't go,' she murmured and opened her eyes. She turned onto her back and pulled herself up on her pillows with her elbows. She reached out for the glass of water on her bedside table and gulped several mouthfuls. Then she looked directly at me.

'I owe you an apology, Macrinus,' she said, each word tumbling on the previous one's heels. 'I acted like an overbearing idiot the other evening.' She looked down at her bedclothes. 'I'm so sorry. You are my oldest friend and I treated you like shit.'

She looked up at me again with an expression so abject I wanted to cradle her in my arms and soothe the anxiety away. And I thought I saw fear there as well.

'Please say something,' she whispered.

'Accepted.' What a stupid thing to say. She'd think I was cold, unfeeling. I pulled a chair over to the side of her bed, sat and took her hand. 'I didn't mean that to sound abrupt. But what did I do that made you so angry with me? And say those things about Dolcia?'

Her cheeks flamed and she took her lower lip in between her teeth. She shook her head.

'You were brilliant saving us from those thugs,' I said, encouragingly. 'We were so lucky you came along.'

She tried to pull her hand away, but I held on to it. Some instinct told me this was make or break.

'I— I was feeling out of sorts,' she mumbled. 'A post-action reaction.'

'Is that the real reason?'

'Um, yes.'

I knew she wasn't being truthful with me. Worse, she wasn't being truthful with herself.

'Allegra, look at me.' She glanced at me, away, then back at me. 'Now we have to talk this through.' I took a deep breath. 'We've been friends for most of our lives, but if we're honest with ourselves, it's become more than that, hasn't it?'

'Oh!'

Her eyes widened. Was it in surprise or dismay? Was I completely wrong?

Gods.

Allegra

Juno, what was Macrinus saying? That he loved me? No, it couldn't be true. My heart leapt inside me and pounded so hard I could hardly hear myself think. No, he was just feeling sorry for me. He'd seen I'd had a crush on him for years and was trying to let me down gently. I daren't think he meant anything else. Dad had said to seize the day, but I dreaded Macrinus's rejection. I'd rather die. He looked so serious. Surely love meant smiles and joy, not this agony.

'You are very dear to me, Macrinus,' I began. 'I couldn't get through anything without you. I hate quarrelling with you. You're my best friend.'

'Best friend? That's it?' His face clouded over. 'Nothing more?'

'What do you mean?'

'Do you really have no feelings, Allegra, or are you just cruel? A tease? Can't you see that I love you? And have done for years. That I want to be with you for the rest of my life?'

I stared at him. Now he looked furious. His face was stiff with hurt. He'd really meant it.

'No, no. I didn't understand,' I cried out.

But he'd dropped my hand, turned and gone.

I lay awake for the next two hours alternating between feeling incompetent and heartless. A sore pain had taken root in my chest. I'd driven away the only man I could ever love. Other people seemed to find dating and loving so easy. Sergilia changed men every month; I couldn't keep up with her. But she always remained on good terms with them afterwards. What was wrong with me? Tears dribbled out of the sides of my eyes. My throat was sore and my ankle was throbbing. Mars, I was pathetic.

A knock at the door, then my mother entered with a couple of books in her free hand.

'Here, something to help pass the time.'

I smiled my thanks and sniffed. She passed me a box of tissues.

'That was only an excuse. I have to talk to you, Allegra, and you're probably going to get upset.'

I swallowed hard. Was Fausta going to throw me out after all? That would make my life completely perfect.

'I've just had a long talk with Junia.'

'Junia?'

'She came to see me an hour ago, distraught. She'd had a serious row with Macrinus in which he told her where she could go.'

'What? No. He adores her and she him.'

'Exactly. It was about you.' She kept her face neutral, but her eyes seemed to bore into me.

I grasped the base of my throat.

'What— what do you mean?'

'You really don't know?' She took my hand. 'I know you live in a focused world, Allegra, and you're very serious about all that you do. You've always been on the solemn side, keeping your own thoughts and feelings contained.' She stroked my forehead. 'But sometimes we have to let our feelings out and deal with them. I was worried when you were young and that bastard Petronax had you, the twins and Nonna arrested. Then you were so contained and grown up when your father was going through his troubles and Great Nonna died. I was so proud of my capable and strong daughter. I thought I knew how much I loved you before then, but somehow, it grew even stronger. Then the horror of Nicola. And you coped even then. No, you were heroic. Now you are a shining star in your career.'

I nearly choked.

'Please stop, Mama,' I whispered.

'Take the bouquet, Allegra. There aren't that many in life.' She raised an eyebrow and smiled at me, then her face became solemn. 'But there's one area in which you're pretty weak.'

I went to protest, but she put her hand up.

'Hear me out. Junia is one of the old guard, tough as teak. She went through the Great Rebellion with Great Nonna.'

'Yes, I know.' And she never let the younger generation forget it.

'It takes a fair amount to rile and to stymie her. Macrinus has succeeded in doing both. He was in a towering rage at lunchtime. She told him to calm down but he let it all out. It seems some very unfortunate words were exchanged.'

Gods. Macrinus loved his mother. What the hell had he said?

'It seems he's been burning a candle for you all his life, but kept it contained. Junia told him to look elsewhere, that you'd partner with somebody from one of the other Twelve Families. He then lashed out at her and told her she didn't understand anything. I have to say I was surprised. It sounds as if he's behaving like an adolescent on his first crush.'

'No, he's very sensible and mature,' I burst out. 'Far more so than I will ever be. She must have said something really horrible.'

'Really? I don't think so. Here's how I see it. His feelings for you are intense. He's behaved very well. It was only when your father told me about your conversation at the PGSF sick bay that I caught on.'

'That was private! He had no right to tell you.'

'Sure,' she said drily. 'You suppose your father would put that before sharing how distressed you were. And still are.' She pressed my hand. 'I know you keep your feelings very much to yourself, darling, but this isn't the time. Let go, Allegra. Open up your heart. Macrinus is deeply in love with you. He's the steady type. Whatever may happen in the future, you'd be the biggest fool in Roma Nova to let him slip through your hands.'

I bowed my head.

'What are you afraid of, darling? Don't you love him?'

'Yes,' I sniffed.

'Then what?'

'I don't know what to do,' I whispered.

She pulled me to her. I relaxed into her warm hug.

'Just be yourself. Tell him what you feel. And trust him.'

The next day, I hobbled down to the old study. It was Great Nonna's really. Volumes of leather-bound books huddled on shelves and looked impressive, but now her old desk supported a state-of-the-art fibre-connected desktop computer. Her sofa, easy chairs and coffee table had survived the rebellion in the eighties and looked like a time capsule of their own. But they were wonderfully comfortable, like sitting in a soft cocoon. I'd laid my crutch down at the side and limped over to the sofa. Coffee was on the way and so was Macrinus.

How in Hades could I face him? My hands were trembling, but I took some deep breaths to calm myself. The door opened and he stood on the threshold, the tray in his hands. He nudged the door shut with his heel, then came over and deposited the tray on the table. In silence, and without looking at me, he poured two cups and added milk and sugar in mine. He handed me the cup, then sat back in the easy chair opposite and waited.

It was unbearable. Brown shadows circled his eyes. And despite his effort to look relaxed his shoulders were hunched up. He sat with his legs crossed, one swinging slightly to and fro, and he was tapping the chair arm with his fingers. Had I caused this tension? Gods. I just wanted to put my arms around him and comfort him, to shelter him from the world and from my stupid self.

'Macrinus,' I started. 'I'm so confused. I was clumsy and rude yesterday. I don't know what to do. The last thing in the world I wanted to do was to hurt you.'

'No, I owe you an apology,' he said, his face tight. 'It's plain to see you don't have the same strength of feeling for me as I do for you. I won't bother you again.'

I gasped.

'No, no, I didn't mean that!' I said. 'You usually know me so well. As well as my parents do. Better. I'd be devastated if you left me now. Please don't pull away from me.'

'Give me a good reason not to.'

Now his face was hard, like Dad's when he was stubborn. Or hurt.

'Because... because I need you.'

'Need?'

'I'm not clever or smooth like you. I don't know how to say this. Help me.'

'What do you want to say, Allegra?'

'Why are you making this so difficult for me?'

'I'm not.'

'You're making a damned good job of it,' I retorted.

He stopped tapping his fingers and looked away for an instant.

'Do you remember when you were sixteen and I came back from London?' he said, fixing his eyes on my face. 'You were in the atrium. You just stared at me. I saw intense longing in your eyes, but you couldn't utter a word. I was transfixed by the strength of your emotion. But you were so young, I kept back. But over the years, I've seen that look in your eyes many times. And recently it's been more intense. Don't you know what that means? What's behind it?'

'That I'm pleased to see my friend,' I mumbled into my coffee.

'Stop pretending to yourself, Allegra,' he said softly. 'Say what you really feel.'

I glanced at him. His eyes were almost black and he was leaning forward. I put my hand out. He stood and took it, then kissed the palm. I pulled him onto the sofa and encircled him with my arms. My heart thudded and a warmth spread through me. I was home.

He tipped my chin up with his free hand and kissed me gently on my lips. Gods. It was electric. I bent towards him again, but he drew back a few centimetres.

'Can you say it now?' He studied my face.

'Don't push it, Macrinus.'

'Try.' He smiled at me. 'I know you can. You're brave, even when fighting yourself.'

I swallowed hard.

'I— I think I must love you,' I said nervously. My stomach clenched with fear at being so open and vulnerable.

'Not a bad start.' He chuckled. 'Don't be embarrassed about talking of love. Just speak from your heart.'

I stared down, but he put his fingers under my chin and brought my face up to his.

'Shall we try and progress from there?' he said softly. 'I reckon we'll need at least two decades to work on this.'

'Shall we agree on three as a minimum?' I said and kissed him hard.

WOULD YOU LEAVE A REVIEW?

I hope you enjoyed ROMA NOVA EXTRA, the danger, adventures and passions of the past, present and future.

If you did, I'd really appreciate it if you would write a few words of review on the site where you purchased this book.

Reviews will really help ROMA NOVA EXTRA to feature more prominently on retailer sites and let more people into the world of Roma Nova.

Very many thanks!

HISTORICAL NOTE

What if Julius Caesar had taken notice of the warning that assassins wanted to murder him on the ides of March? Suppose Elizabeth I had married and had children? If plague hadn't rampaged through Europe in the fourteenth century? Or if Christianity had remained a Middle Eastern minor cult, or Napoleon had won at Waterloo?

The concept of a society with Roman values surviving for fifteen centuries is meant to intrigue. ROMA NOVA EXTRA reveals a few episodes in the past as well as revisiting favourite characters in the present and near future. I have dropped background 'history' of Roma Nova into the stories only where it impacts on the story. Nobody likes a history lesson in the middle of a thriller! But if you are interested in how the mysterious Roma Nova survived into the 21st century, read on...

What happened in our timeline

Our timeline may of course, turn out to be somebody else's alternative one as shown in Philip K. Dick's *The Grasshopper Lies Heavy*, the story within the story in *The Man in the High Castle*. Nothing is fixed. But for the sake of convenience I take ours as the default.

The Western Roman Empire didn't 'fall' in a cataclysmic event as often portrayed in film and television; it localised and dissolved like chain mail fragmenting into separate links, giving way to rump provinces, city states and petty kingdoms. The Eastern Roman Empire survived until the Fall of Constantinople in 1453 to the Ottoman Empire.

Some scholars think that Christianity fatally weakened the traditional Roman way of life. Emperor Constantine's personal conversion to Christianity in AD 313 was a turning point. By late AD 394, his several times successor, Theodosius, had banned all traditional Roman religious practice, closed and destroyed temples and dismissed all priests. The sacred flame that had burned in the College of Vestals for over a thousand years was extinguished and the vestal virgins expelled. The Altar of Victory, said to guard the fortune of Rome, was hauled away from the Senate building and disappeared from history.

The Roman senatorial families pleaded for religious tolerance, but Theodosius made any pagan practice, even dropping a pinch of incense on a family altar in a private home, into a capital offence. And his 'religious police', driven by the austere and ambitious bishop Ambrosius of Milan, became increasingly active in pursuing pagans.

The alternative Roma Nova timeline

In AD 395, three months after Theodosius's final decree banning all non-Christian religious activity, four hundred Romans loyal to the old gods, and so in danger of execution, trekked north out of Italy to a semi-mountainous area similar to modern Slovenia. Led by Senator Apulius at the head of twelve prominent families, they established a colony based initially on land owned by Apulius's Celtic father-in-law. By purchase, alliance and conquest, this grew into Roma Nova.

Norman Davies in *Vanished Kingdoms: The History of Half-Forgotten Europe* reminds us that:

> ...in order to survive, newborn states need to possess a set of viable internal organs, including a functioning executive, a defence force, a revenue system and a diplomatic force. If they possess none of these

things, they lack the means to sustain an autonomous existence and they perish before they can breathe and flourish.

I would add history, willpower and adaptability as essential factors. Roma Nova survived by changing its social structure; as men constantly fought to defend the new colony, women took over the social, political and economic roles, weaving new power and influence networks based on family structures. Given the unstable, dangerous times in Roma Nova's first few hundred years, daughters as well as sons had to put on armour and heft swords to defend their homeland and their way of life. Fighting for survival side by side with brothers and fathers reinforced women's roles and status.

The Roma Novans never allowed the incursion of monotheistic, paternalistic religions; they'd learnt that lesson from old Rome. Service to the state was valued higher than personal advantage, echoing Roman Republican virtues, and the women heading the families guarded and enhanced these values to provide a core philosophy throughout the centuries. Inheritance passed from these powerful women to their daughters and granddaughters.

Roma Nova's continued existence has been favoured by three factors: the discovery and exploitation of high-grade silver in their mountains, their efficient technology, and their flexible but robust response to any threat. Under pressure from the Eastern Romans, they sent an envoy to stop the Norman invasion of England (as you can read here).

Remembering the Fall of Constantinople, Roma Novan troops assisted at the Battle of Vienna in 1683 to halt the Ottoman advance into Europe. Nearly two hundred years later, they used their diplomatic skills to forge an alliance to push Napoleon IV back across the Rhine as he attempted to expand his grandfather's empire.

Prioritising survival, Roma Nova remained neutral in the Great War of the twentieth century which lasted from 1925 to 1935. The Greater German Empire was broken up afterwards into its former small kingdoms, duchies and counties; some became republics. Today, the tiny country of Roma Nova has become one of the highest per capita income states in the world.

ROMA NOVA EXTRA is a collection of short stories; some reveal and illuminate events in history, others give glimpses into the modern characters. You don't have to have read any of the series to enjoy these stories. But I hope you'll be tempted to...

THE ROMA NOVA THRILLER SERIES

The Carina Mitela adventures

INCEPTIO

Early 21st century. Terrified after a kidnap attempt, New Yorker Karen Brown, has a harsh choice – being terminated by government enforcer Renschman or fleeing to Roma Nova, her dead mother's homeland in Europe. Founded sixteen hundred years ago by Roman exiles and ruled by women, it gives Karen safety, at a price. But Renschman follows and sets a trap she has no option but to enter.

CARINA – *A novella*

Carina Mitela is still an inexperienced officer in the Praetorian Guard Special Forces of Roma Nova. Disgraced for a disciplinary offence, she is sent out of everybody's way to bring back a traitor from the Republic of Quebec. But when she discovers a conspiracy reaching into the highest levels of Roma Nova, what price is personal danger against fulfilling the mission?

PERFIDITAS

Falsely accused of conspiracy, 21st century Praetorian Carina Mitela flees into the criminal underworld. Hunted by the security services and traitors alike, she struggles to save her beloved Roma Nova as well as her own life.

But the ultimate betrayal is waiting for her…

SUCCESSIO

21st century Praetorian Carina Mitela's attempt to resolve a past family indiscretion is spiralling into a nightmare. Convinced her beloved husband has deserted her, and with her enemy holding a gun to the imperial heir's head, Carina has to make the hardest decision of her life.

The Aurelia Mitela adventures

AURELIA

Late 1960s. Sent to Berlin to investigate silver smuggling, former Praetorian Aurelia Mitela barely escapes a near-lethal trap. Her old enemy is at the heart of all her troubles and she pursues him back home to Roma Nova but he strikes at her most vulnerable point – her young daughter.

INSURRECTIO

Early 1980s. Caius Tellus, the charismatic leader of a rising nationalist movement, threatens to destroy Roma Nova.

Aurelia Mitela, ex-Praetorian and imperial councillor, attempts to counter the growing fear and instability. But it may be too late to save Roma Nova from meltdown and herself from destruction by her lifelong enemy....

RETALIO

Early 1980s Vienna. Aurelia Mitela chafes at her enforced exile. She barely escaped from a near fatal shooting by her nemesis, Caius Tellus, who grabbed power in Roma Nova.

Aurelia is determined to liberate her homeland. But Caius's manipulations have ensured that she is ostracised by her fellow exiles. Powerless and vulnerable, Aurelia fears she will never see Roma Nova again.

ROMA NOVA EXTRA

A collection of short stories

Four historical and four present day and a little beyond

A young tribune sent to a backwater in 370 AD for practising the wrong religion, his lonely sixty-fifth descendant labours in the 1980s to reconstruct her country. A Roma Novan imperial councillor attempting to stop the Norman invasion of England in 1066, her 21st century Praetorian descendant flounders as she searches for her own happiness.

Some are love stories, some are lessons learned, some resolve tensions and unrealistic visions, some are plain adventures, but above all, they are stories of people in dilemmas and conflict, and their courage and effort to resolve them.

www.ingramcontent.com/pod-product-compliance
Lightning Source LLC
LaVergne TN
LVHW041704060526
838201LV00043B/568